Surprise at Logan School

Connie Griffith and her family live in Boone, North Carolina. She and her husband serve at the headquarters of Africa Evangelical Fellowship. This is her first series of American children's novels.

The Tootie McCarthy Series

BOOK 2

Surprise at Logan School

Connie Griffith

Published by Baker Books
a division of Baker Book House Company
P.O. Box 6287, Grand Rapids, MI 49516-6287

Second printing, August 1994

Printed in the United States of America

Library of Congress Cataloging-in-Publication Data

Griffith, Connie.
Surprise at Logan School / Connie Griffith.
p. cm. — (The Tootie McCarthy series ; bk. 2)
Sequel to: The unexpected weapon.
Sequel: Secret behind locked doors.
Summary: In the winter of 1927, thirteen-year-old Tootie McCarthy worries about her family's economic situation, the upcoming Christmas play at school, and the Gypsies who have camped near her home in St. Paul, Minnesota.
ISBN 0-8010-3856-1
[1. Irish Americans—Fiction. 2. Christian life—Fiction. 3. Gypsies—Fiction. 4. Schools—Fiction. 5. Family life—Fiction.] I. Title. II. Series: Griffith, Connie. Tootie McCarthy series ; bk. 2.
PZ7.G88175Su 1993
[Fic]—dc20 93-13975

Scripture quotations are from the King James Version of the Bible.

To Gypsies
and all others
who have experienced prejudice.

Tootie scooted to the edge of the big oak chair in Mr. Harris's office until the scuffed toes of her brown shoes touched the floor. Her sister, Pearl, had also been called to the principal's office, and the two sisters sat nervously side by side.

"Now you listen to me, young ladies," Mr. Harris began as he shuffled through a stack of papers on his desk. "You McCarthys are causing a lot of trouble around here, and I don't like it. To be honest, we haven't had this much disturbance at Logan School since I came here five years ago." He took a deep breath and leaned back in his swivel chair, folding his hands over his protruding belly. "What do you girls have to say for yourselves?"

Pearl kept her head lowered and continued fidgeting with her fingers. Her pale skin was drained of any color.

Tootie stared at her fifteen-year-old sister, hoping she would somehow apologize for causing so much trouble. Finally Tootie broke the strained silence. "Sir, Pearl is sorry for being in the street meetings last week and upsetting the whole school. She won't do it again. I promise!"

"Is that a fact?" Mr. Harris asked. He leaned forward over his desk. "Since those disgraceful displays last week with Pearl's banjo playing and her friend's frightening speeches, the whole school is abuzz with gossip."

Pearl still didn't say anything, but Tootie thought she saw her sister's skin turn even paler.

"Sorry, Sir," Tootie murmured.

Mr. Harris kept looking back and forth from one sister to the other. "There are rumors flying all around the halls about the both of you. And, I might add, there are literally dozens of stories about what happened to that street preacher over the weekend. What did that young man call himself anyway? Banjo Ed?"

"Yes, sir," Tootie said, and glanced sideways at Pearl who once again was on the verge of tears. Since Pearl's boyfriend, Banjo Ed, as he liked to be called, had fled the scene Sunday afternoon, she had been withdrawn and depressed. Banjo Ed had pretended to be a Christian. He had even preached frightening sermons right across the street from the school for all the students to hear. But Banjo Ed was trying to scare people and then take their money. Somehow he had tricked Pearl and she had foolishly joined him in his sick scheme.

Tootie scooted even closer to the edge of the chair and planted her feet firmly on the floor. She took a deep breath and held it for a second, trying desperately to calm her quivering voice. "I can assure you that this school won't be bothered by Banjo Ed anymore. My sister . . . er . . . she won't be seeing him or—or joining with him to scare the students into giving money, I promise!"

"Now that *is* good news!" Mr. Harris exclaimed, and his eyebrows shot halfway up his forehead. "I don't want that young man coming around here again. I want to see our school settle down after all this excitement, and I especially want to see you Irish girls applying yourselves more diligently to your studies."

"Yes, sir," Tootie replied, wondering what in the world being Irish had to do with anything.

Pearl kept staring at the floor.

Mr. Harris turned his full attention to Tootie. "You're a ninth grader in Miss Penick's class, correct?"

Tootie nodded. She looked directly at the principal as she nervously traced the outline of the patch on her yellow gingham dress.

"I've heard the strangest stories about how you, Tootie McCarthy, single-handedly dealt with Banjo Ed. And I hear you did it right in broad daylight on Washington Street. Now, I'm sure these reports are false; they're too ridiculous to be true. No thirteen-year-old girl could handle such a situation with a bully like that. Yes, it is all quite ridiculous, to say the least."

Tootie stared at the brass pen set on Mr. Harris's desk, trying not to blink. She squeezed the material of her dress between her fingers, hoping he wouldn't ask what really did happen.

"And another thing, young lady," he continued, "your

teacher, Miss Penick, has reported to me that you are having extreme difficulty with your mathematics. She is most concerned about your lack of progress, and she assures me she has done all she can to assist you."

Tootie pushed her naturally curly brown hair away from her face. "I'm trying, sir. Honest. Joey Staddler is helping me."

"Joey who? Oh, yes . . . the Staddler boy. He's quite a good student. Well, make sure you start applying yourself more diligently. You're in ninth grade now and your work isn't going to get any easier from here on out."

"Yes, sir," Tootie replied.

Just then they heard a loud noise outside and Mr. Harris hurried to the window. He smacked his lips against his teeth in disgust. "I can't believe the city is allowing that confounded construction project to take place so close to this high school. 'Progress!' the mayor says. 'This is 1927 and there's no time like the present to build.'"

Mr. Harris shook his head as he mimicked the mayor's comments and then continued more thoughtfully. "Well, these are financially good times for a lot of people. But I still don't like all that confounded commotion so close to my school. Most disturbing for my students." He stayed at the window for a long time, irritably shaking his bald head.

Tootie glanced over at Pearl and shrugged her shoulders. The minutes ticked by on the big clock which hung above the office door. The McCarthy sisters sat quietly, hardly daring to breathe.

Finally Mr. Harris spoke as he continued looking out the window. "I can think of only one thing that would be worse than all this construction—and that's Gypsies. If the Gypsies came to town and parked their caravans here, it would be disastrous!"

Tootie gasped. She had heard a lot about Gypsies but had never seen any. She'd even heard stories about how they put spells on people and how they'd steal anything they could get their hands on, even children. Her mother had instructed her that if she ever saw a Gypsy, to run and hide. Tootie's whole body quivered at the thought of such people coming to St. Paul, Minnesota, and parking next to her school.

Mr. Harris turned around and looked surprised. Once again his eyebrows shot up. "Oh . . . are you McCarthys still here? Well, get back to your respective classrooms immediately. And no more tomfoolery from either one of you."

"Yes, sir," the sisters replied.

"And squelch all of these silly stories surrounding your heroics concerning Banjo Ed. You understand?" He stared hard at Tootie.

"Yes," Tootie said in a nervous tone, "I . . . I understand."

"Good! Now, let's hope this is the end of an extremely distasteful experience in the life of my school. It's been most disturbing." Mr. Harris turned his back on them and once again stared out the window, letting his warm breath cloud the cold pane.

Tootie and Pearl knew they were excused. Quickly they left the office.

As soon as they reached the long hallway, Pearl turned on Tootie as if she were a cat ready to pounce. "What do you mean by telling him I won't be seeing Banjo Ed ever again? Maybe I will!"

"Oh, Pearl!" Tootie said, totally exasperated. "How can you possibly want him back after the way he talked to you and tricked you? And how, for pity's sake, could you stand him after he shoved our little brother into the gutter?" Tootie's thoughts churned and twisted like a whirlwind as she recalled seeing her eight-year-old retarded brother sprawled in the gutter with huge tears streaming down his cheeks. "Oh, Pearl, that boyfriend of yours could have hurt Buddy!" There was a strangled catch in Tootie's voice.

"Well," Pearl defended, "we did all gang up on Banjo Ed . . . especially you, Tootie. I still can't believe what you did to him." Pearl stomped her foot.

"Pearl! Keep your voice down! Haven't you got us in enough trouble already?" Tootie quickly scanned the hallway.

"Me?" Pearl almost shouted. She straightened her shoulders and looked down her narrow nose. "It was you and that Joey Staddler who took our banjos and all of our money. It's your fault. And then you had to go and squirt Banjo Ed with all that vinegar! Oh, Tootie, how could you!"

Tootie was so mad she couldn't talk; all she could do was stare openmouthed at her sister. *Why doesn't Pearl mention how we gave everything back? How could she forget how Banjo Ed acted?*

Pearl's voice calmed slightly as they turned the corner in the hall. "Maybe Banjo Ed didn't mean all those bad things he said. I've been thinking . . ." Pearl stopped in mid-sentence and stood there deep in thought with her lower lip jutting out in a giant pout.

Tootie felt like bopping her on the head.

Pearl continued, "I've been thinking, Tootie, that maybe we misunderstood Banjo Ed . . . I mean Eddie. Maybe he'll come back and . . . and everything will be all right again."

Tootie couldn't believe that being in love could make her sister so stupid.

Pearl was about to continue when her front teeth, which were attached to a plastic plate on the roof of her mouth, moved downward, revealing a space between the false teeth and Pearl's gums. Quickly Pearl clapped her hand over her mouth and tears welled up in her eyes. "I hate these stupid teeth! What other teenager has false teeth? I hate them! I hate them! I hate them!"

Several tears escaped and slowly trickled down Pearl's pale face. "Banjo Ed promised he'd give me the money to get my teeth fixed if I'd help him with the street meetings," she cried. "He promised! He told me that if I played my banjo and sang he would give me the money we collected so I could go to the dentist. That's why I did it."

"I know," Tootie soothed. "He tricked you."

"Oh, Tootie, I want my teeth fixed! I just hate it when they slip and slide all around." Pearl hiccupped several times and wiped her eyes.

"I know, Pearl. I'm sorry." Tootie reached up and hugged her sister. "There . . . there now. Maybe we can all work together as a family and earn enough money so you can go to a good dentist."

Pearl cried even harder. "You know how it is, Tootie. Mama and Daddy can't afford anything. We're getting poorer by the day."

Tootie thought of what Mr. Harris had said about this being a good time for most businesses. Yet, for some reason, their parents' bakery business was failing.

They clung together for a long time. Finally a student came out of a nearby classroom and they quickly separated. "We'd better get to class," Tootie whispered. "I'll see you right after school and we'll walk home together."

Pearl nodded and wiped her tears.

It seemed natural for Tootie to be encouraging her older sister. She'd done a lot of that lately. Tootie turned toward Miss Penick's room and opened the door.

"Just in time for mathematics," Miss Penick greeted. "And by the way, we hope Mr. Harris gave you a good talking to. There's been entirely too much gossip going around this school about you and that family of yours. You Irish folk," Miss Penick said with great disgust, "you're always causing trouble."

Several students giggled.

Miss Penick frowned. "Enough, class! We want none

of that in here." And then she turned back to Tootie. "Get to your seat, young lady, and take out your mathematics book. You need all the instruction you can get." Miss Penick tapped her big foot irritably.

Tootie hurried to her seat in the front row and jerked open her desk to take out paper and book. She hated the way Miss Penick always singled her out.

Joey leaned forward and poked the back of Tootie's arm, mumbling something under his breath. She still found it hard to believe that months earlier they had been sworn enemies and now Joey Staddler was her closest friend. The events of the past weeks had bonded them together in a special way.

For the remainder of the day, Tootie found it almost impossible to concentrate on her schoolwork. There was a lot on her mind: her sister's depression, her brother's slowness, their family's creeping poverty, and now the problem of trying to stop the gossip about how she, a little Irish girl, single-handedly defeated the big brute, Banjo Ed.

The giant machines outside were making grinding noises as they dug into the ground in preparation for a new building. Tootie shivered as she remembered Mr. Harris's comments about Gypsies. She quickly added the threat of Gypsies to her list of worries. With anxious fingers, she pulled her brown cardigan until it doubled over in front and then folded her arms across her flat chest. She continued hugging herself while staring down at her mathematics book.

Finally the dismissal bell rang and Miss Penick said,

"Wait class! We have an announcement to make before you leave."

Everyone hushed.

Miss Penick smiled and her long, bird-like nose turned red with obvious excitement. "As a faculty, we have discussed the upcoming Christmas play. We are already into the first week of December, so we don't have much time before the thirteenth—that's the night of the performance. Please tell your parents and be sure to write it on your calendars. Remember now, December 13—that's the important day—because we, as the ninth-grade class, have been chosen to do the school drama!"

The class cheered.

Miss Penick continued, "The upper classmen will be singing in a choir and playing their instruments, but we will be doing the actual play with costumes and all."

Irene, the most popular girl in class, let out a little squeal. "What fun. I love dressing up in fancy clothes. Someday I'm going to be an actress."

Tootie felt another panic rising within her. She knew that the students who took part in the Christmas play had to provide their own costumes. She also knew her family would not be able to afford one for her.

Joey leaned forward and whispered, "Hey, Tootie, you'd make a g-great angel!"

In spite of her worries, Tootie turned around and smiled at Joey. "Come on, you know Miss Penick won't choose me for that part. I don't think she sees me as the angel type."

Joey pushed his straight hair out of his eyes. “I don’t know. W-why not? You’d make a g-great angel.” He sounded and looked serious.

Tootie’s heart began to race. She shook her head as if to chase away the thought. Then she giggled and whispered back to Joey, “I would make the most unlikely angel Logan School ever had!”

As soon as Miss Penick dismissed the class, the ninth graders started filing out. Joey stood up behind Tootie and put on his black-and-white plaid jacket. Tootie noticed that he looked tired. His straight brown hair hung in front of his eyes and one of his suspenders was twisted. He plopped his hat toward the back of his head. "Hey, you sure stayed in the p-principal's office for a long time this afternoon.

"I know," Tootie said as she slipped into her hand-me-down wool coat. It had a few moth holes right in front that Mother had missed the last time she did the mending. Tootie quickly tied her red scarf under her chin.

"Well, don't keep it a s-secret," Joey urged. "What did the old b-baldy have to say?"

"Joey!" Tootie laughed. "That's awful!"

"I know," Joey admitted and smiled. "Come on, Tootie, does Mr. Harris know what really happened last weekend between you and Banjo Ed?"

"No, he's just heard the gossip like everyone else. But I did promise him that we've all seen the last of him."

"Good! I hope s-so!"

"And guess what! Mr. Harris wants me to put a stop to the rumors that are going around the school."

"How can you do that? You c-c-can't control what people say."

Tootie shrugged. "We'll have to try, Joey. We'll have to ignore all the comments about Pearl's old boyfriend. And let's not answer any more questions. Maybe that'll work. Mama always says that sometimes the less said the better."

Joey shook his head. "It's w-worth a try."

"Hey," Tootie said, completely changing the subject, "what did you think of Miss Penick's announcement? Do you want to be in the Christmas play?"

"Sure do. But I don't want an acting p-part or anything like that. I want to do the p-props or lights or help with the s-s-sound effects."

Tootie's thin lips spread into a relieved smile as she nodded. "Maybe I'll do that, too. I don't want to have to get dressed up in some stupid old costume or anything."

"Oh, come on, Tootie. Miss Penick isn't going to let girls do the lights or p-props. That's boys' stuff."

Tootie stiffened.

Joey didn't seem to notice her response. "Besides," he continued, "I was telling the truth when I s-said you'd make a good angel."

Tootie good-naturedly slapped him on the arm and they both laughed.

Before they reached the edge of the school grounds, the cold wind was whipping their faces. Tootie quickly tucked her hair firmly under her scarf and pulled her coat collar higher. She was about to comment on the terrible weather when she spotted Pearl standing by the steps of the Alliance Bible Church which sat kitty-corner from the school. They hurried to join her.

"Hi," Tootie greeted.

Pearl's only response was to turn and head down Washington Street toward home.

Tootie looked at Joey and shrugged. "I hate it when my sister gets in one of her moods," she whispered.

It wasn't long before they reached the Specialty Pie Bakery where the McCarthys lived. Pearl was just ahead of them.

When they came to the outside steps to the small family apartment upstairs, Tootie turned to Joey. "Do you want to come with Buddy and me? I'm taking him to play catch in that old abandoned field we found."

"Today? In this weather?"

Tootie laughed. "Sure."

"Yeah, I'll come," Joey said. "But I'll have to run h-home and ask." Joey's parents owned the Staddler Grocery Store which stood directly opposite the Specialty Pie Bakery. The Staddlers occupied the rooms in back of the grocery. "I'll be right back," Joey yelled as he turned and darted across the busy street.

"Why don't you come, too?" Tootie asked Pearl as she hurried up the apartment steps behind her sister. *She's not the softball type,* Tootie thought, *but it's worth a try.* "Come with us," Tootie encouraged. "We'll have lots of fun."

"Oh, really!" Pearl pouted. "When have you ever seen me play ball? I hate sports! No . . . I just want to go lie down."

Tootie knew that their father was probably down in the bakery talking with customers. He was always cheerful, and Pearl enjoyed sitting around in the bakery after school talking with him. "Why don't you go see Father?" Tootie suggested. "He'll cheer you up."

"No, I don't want to be with anybody," Pearl sulked, "not even Daddy. I'm so lonesome for Banjo Ed."

Stop feeling sorry for yourself, Tootie wanted to say. *A lot of other girls have lost their boyfriends, and some have even been fooled like you were. It's not the end of the world!*

But Tootie didn't say a word. *Besides,* she thought, *Pearl would never listen to any advice from me.*

Quickly Tootie opened the apartment door and yelled, "Mama, we're home."

Eve McCarthy stuck her head around the kitchen door and smiled at her daughters. "I'm making soup," she explained, holding up a big potato. Her graying hair was pulled into its usual tight bun, but Tootie thought she noticed a more relaxed look around mother's deep-set eyes. Maybe she was relieved that Pearl had come home right after school and wasn't running around with Banjo Ed anymore.

"Can I take Buddy for a walk?" Tootie asked. She knew the answer would be a thankful *Yes!* Eight-year-old Buddy was a handful. He needed constant tending that often wore Mother to a frazzle, and Father didn't want Buddy in the bakery. He claimed that the customers felt uncomfortable when Buddy was around.

"That'd be nice," Mother said and smiled warmly at Tootie. "Buddy needs to get out for a while."

Pearl hurried to the bedroom after hardly greeting Mother.

Eve frowned slightly and then continued. "Tootie, be sure you take your brother to the bathroom before you leave. Also, make sure he dresses warm enough, hat and all. There's a real nip in the air and you know how quickly our Buddy catches cold."

"Yes, Mama," Tootie replied and quickly turned to the living room. Buddy was sitting on the floor in the middle of a small scatter rug which was pushed close to a steam radiator. He was fiddling with his shoes.

"Toooотie! Toot, Toot, Toot," he greeted and awkwardly rose to his feet. He held his small round head to one side. His squinty eyes almost disappeared into his rosy cheeks as he grinned.

Tootie hurried over to her brother and gave him a big hug.

He patted her roughly and laid his head tenderly in the crook of her neck.

She let him rest his head for a minute and then she suggested, "Let's go play catch, Buddy Boy."

She'd said the magic word, because Buddy began jumping up and down. "Catch," he said and thrust out his stubby arms.

On impulse, Tootie hugged him again. His simple pleasure in life was so refreshing. It took pitifully little to please him. *Maybe things would be easier if everyone were like Buddy,* Tootie thought.

He shoved her away and yanked at the knotted rope which held up his baggy trousers.

"All right," she giggled, "I'll take you to the bathroom and then we'll go play."

Five minutes later they were both dressed warmly in their coats, scarves, and hats. They headed down the apartment steps and found Joey waiting for them at the bottom.

The three of them leaned against the wind as they walked toward the outskirts of town and the old abandoned field. Tootie had the softball in her coat pocket, and she took it out and tossed it in the air. "Remember when we hated each other?" she said to Joey.

He reached out and caught the ball. "I was just th-thinking about the same thing." He was also remembering how he used to tease Tootie all the time about her retarded brother. Joey looked at Buddy and yelled, "Hey, you w-want to race to the field?"

They started running. Tootie could tell that Joey was slowing his pace to keep in step with Buddy's clumsy gait.

"Wait up!" Tootie yelled and ran after them.

Joey looked at Tootie as they jogged along. "My parents have decided you don't have to pay for all that vinegar you used when you squirted Banjo Ed. After I explained what happened, they said they were p-proud of you for putting a stop to that bully."

Tootie frantically nodded her head toward Buddy

and motioned for Joey to keep his voice down. She didn't want Buddy to be reminded of what had happened and get upset.

But Buddy wasn't paying any attention to them. He kept hollering, "Catch! Catch! Catch!" all the way to the open field.

Later that night after bowls of thick potato soup and two hours of homework, Tootie stretched out in bed to her full four feet ten inches. The full winter moon cast weird shadows across the walls and ceiling. Pearl was lying quietly on the other side of their double bed, and Buddy was snoring across the room. His snores and raspy breathing broke the stillness.

"How can anyone go to sleep with all that noise?" Pearl whispered. "I wish Mama and Daddy would take Buddy into their bedroom. Good grief, we're teenage girls—almost women! We shouldn't have our little brother sleeping in our bedroom."

Tootie hated it when Pearl complained. It only made matters worse.

"Tootie, are you asleep?"

"No," Tootie answered.

"What are you thinking about?"

Tootie's heart warmed toward her sister. "Oh, I was just thinking about the Christmas program. I hear your class is going to sing and play the music. You're lucky, Pearl. You'll get to bring your banjo."

"I know. I hope I get to play a solo."

Tootie didn't respond. She turned onto her side and

hit her pillow, trying to find a more comfortable position. "You'll probably be chosen to play and sing several solos. You're good."

"Do you know what part you're going to play?" Pearl asked.

"I don't want a part," Tootie said.

Pearl leaned closer. "My teacher said that everyone in the ninth grade is going to get a part. She said it's going to be a big performance and every student is required to participate."

Tootie turned over and faced her sister. "What am I going to do about the costume? You know we can't afford anything like that."

Pearl shrugged. "I hadn't thought about that. Maybe you can just throw something together. If you're a shepherd, you can always wear your bathrobe."

"Oh, Pearl. I wouldn't be caught dead in that old thing!"

"Good grief, you're always so dramatic."

"I am not!"

"You are too!" Pearl said. Then her voice got real quiet. "Tootie, do you think Banjo Ed will come to the Christmas play?"

Tootie's whole body stiffened. She couldn't believe Pearl still wanted to see that street preacher. She quickly turned over, away from Pearl, and covered herself with their blanket.

"I wonder what he's doing," Pearl continued, not one bit put off. "I miss him so much. Maybe he really didn't mean to say all those nasty things to me."

Tootie bit her lower lip.

"You're no fun," Pearl complained. "All I wanted to do was talk."

Tootie still didn't respond, except to breathe a little louder and deeper, hoping Pearl would think she had fallen asleep. She even made her shoulder twitch several times, thinking that would be more convincing.

To be honest, Tootie had wanted to talk. She had wanted to try and figure out what role she could play in the Christmas drama that would not involve an expensive costume. She had wanted to find out what Pearl knew about Gypsies, and to see if she thought they would come to Minnesota in the middle of winter. But all Pearl had on her mind these days was Banjo Ed.

"All right, be like that," Pearl whispered. "I didn't want to talk with you either." Pearl turned over in a huff and yanked the covers off Tootie.

Tootie didn't know what do to. If she pulled the covers back, Pearl would know for sure that she was just pretending to be asleep. The night air was cold. Her parents turned down the steam radiators again to save money. Minutes passed and gooseflesh broke out all over Tootie's slender arms and legs. Finally she heard Pearl's slow, rhythmic breathing. Cautiously she reached over and pulled the blanket.

"I thought so!" Pearl shouted. "You can't trick me, Tootie McCarthy. I knew you weren't asleep."

Tootie still didn't say a word. *Who wants to argue anyway,* she thought. Slowly a smile touched her lips. *Maybe I am growing up after all.* But the smile disappeared as she wiggled further under the blanket and wondered what in the world she was going to do about the Christmas play. *Is God interested in things like this? Does he want us to pray about stuff like costumes for a Christmas play?*

Then she remembered the *first* Christmas day when Jesus, the Son of God, had nothing to wear but rags. Pastor Myers had called them swaddling clothes . . . just strips of linen.

Oh, God, Tootie prayed into her pillow, *I want more than rags. I want a beautiful white angel's gown. I want to have a gorgeous, flowing robe and diamonds in my hair. Oh God, please! That would be so wonderful!*

To her surprise, she began to relax. She snuggled into the saggy mattress and took a slow, deep breath. A smile came to her lips as she began to see herself dancing across the school stage. She could hear the surprised whispers from the audience. "Look, isn't that the poor Irish girl who lives above the bakery?" And others who replied, "Yes, that's Tootie McCarthy. Isn't she beautiful!"

Soon Tootie drifted asleep with a gentle smile still on her face.

Early the next morning, Tootie woke to a bitterly cold room. She reached toward the bottom of her bed and grabbed her old faded bathrobe. Quickly she put it on and then pulled her green knit slippers over her small feet. She got out of bed and checked to see that Buddy was covered. Then she hurried to the window. Frost was heavy on the pane and snow covered everything. Only one automobile, with its headlights shining on the falling snow and icy road, was inching slowly down Washington Street.

Just then Mother opened the bedroom door. "Good morning, Tootie," Eve greeted her. "It's nice to see you up so early. This snow certainly took us by surprise."

"Oh, Mama, doesn't it look beautiful?"

"Yes, dear, that is, if you don't have to be out in it. But what really concerns me is that this kind of weather always lowers the number of customers who come in to buy our pies."

Tootie turned back to stare out the window. "Mama,

have you ever heard of Gypsies coming to a place like this?"

"Gypsies!" Eve exclaimed in a loud whisper and hurried over to the window. "Do you see any?"

"No," Tootie said.

"Gracious, Tootie, you gave me an awful scare. Why on earth are you asking about Gypsies?"

"I've just been wondering about them, that's all. Well, would they?"

"Would they what?" Mother asked, frowning.

"Would Gypsies come here to Minnesota?"

"Well, . . . yes, yes they would. Gypsies travel everywhere. They never settle in one place for very long. I guess that's because they steal everything they get their hands on and then have to make a quick getaway."

"Really?" Tootie gasped in fear.

Eve continued, "I've heard there is a place outside of town where they used to stop every year. But that's been ages ago. Anyway, for some reason they quit coming."

Tootie's hazel eyes grew huge.

Mother chuckled. "But even if that no-good group of wanderers decided to come to town, they certainly wouldn't do it in the dead of winter. No, I don't think you have to worry about that. Besides, they stay in caravans and tents and it's just too cold this time of year. And then with all this snow . . ."

Both Tootie and Mother looked out the window again. "I'm glad it's freezing," Tootie whispered.

Eve chuckled. "You really are worried about Gypsies, aren't you?"

Tootie's light brown curls bounced up and down as she shook her head. "Oh, Mama, I don't worry too much, do I?"

Eve smiled. "Yes, you certainly do. In fact, sometimes I think you invent things to worry about." Reaching out, she hugged her daughter. "But you're a good girl, Tootie. I just think you need to learn to trust God more." Mother's smile softened her words. "I realize, however, that I'm partially to blame for all your worrying because I depend on you entirely too much. And that's a fact."

"Oh, Mama," Tootie said.

Eve hugged her again and then held Tootie at arm's length. "I'm sure you don't have to add Gypsies to your list of worries."

"You're sure?"

"Yes!" Mother said emphatically. "Now, enough of this talk. It's time to wake Buddy and get him dressed for the day. Would you do that for me? I've already made hot porridge. It'll help warm you and Pearl before you start to school. By the way, your father says that this weather will probably keep Mrs. Roseen from getting here to make the pies. Without our baker, I certainly have my work cut out for me."

Eve turned toward the bed. "Up, Pearl. Enough of this lolling around. You have a full day ahead of you." Mother turned to leave the room, saying over her shoulder, "Come on, Tootie, don't just stand there. There's work to be done."

Tootie sighed and quickly flipped on the bedside light

while Pearl got up and stumbled down the hallway to the bathroom. Tootie reached into Buddy's drawer of the bureau, got out a clean handkerchief, and began wiping her brother's nose. It always got crusty during the night.

He pulled away, whining, "Tooootie!"

"Now, Buddy Boy, you've got to start the day with a clean face."

"No," Buddy cried and began thrashing his head back and forth.

Tootie dropped the handkerchief and pulled back the covers. Quickly she helped Buddy out of bed and dressed him in an old pair of Father's underwear, a long-sleeved flannel shirt and his favorite overalls. Tootie let him try to put on his shoes and socks.

All the while, her mind twirled with the thought of Gypsies, a costume for the Christmas play, customers staying away from their bakery because of the weather, and even Pearl's depression over Banjo Ed.

The rest of the morning went as usual for Tootie, except she wore her leggings under her dress and kept them on all day at school even though most of the other girls took theirs off the minute they got into the building. Mr. Harris didn't call her into his office again, and some of the school gossip was already decreasing. *It's amazing,* Tootie thought, *how one day you're the center of attention and the next day no one really cares.*

That afternoon, a few minutes before the dismissal bell, Miss Penick announced, "Class, instead of having you choose which part you want in the Christmas play, we have decided for you."

Several students moaned.

"None of that," Miss Penick said sternly. Then she switched her tone to a high singsong fashion as if she were speaking to a group of babies. "I'm going to walk around the room and hand out your assignments on these cards. No complaining when you receive your part. We've put a lot of thought into this, and we believe we've matched things pretty well, all considered."

Irene whispered loud enough for all to hear, "I want to be an angel. With my long hair, I'd be perfect!"

"Hush!" Miss Penick said and looked around the room. "No talking!" Then the teacher began walking up and down the aisles placing a card, face down, on each desk.

When Irene looked at hers she squealed, "I'm Mary! Whoever thought I'd get the part of *Mary*?" She flipped her long hair proudly and smiled around at her classmates. "Oh, I'm going to have *so* many lines to memorize. This is going to be *so* perfect!"

You've got a lot to learn about Mary! Tootie thought. Then she stared down at her own card, not wanting to turn it over.

Joey whispered, "Hey, I got w-what I wanted. I'm doing the lights. And it says here that I'm also s-s-supposed to help you with your props. What does that mean? W-what's your part, Tootie?"

She looked over her shoulder and whispered, "I don't know."

Joey leaned across and grabbed her card. "Quit being so s-silly."

Tootie tried to snatch her card back, but Joey held it out of reach.

By now, everyone in the classroom was talking, and Miss Penick was having an impossible time getting order.

"Hey, Tootie, you're the head angel!" Joey said excitedly. "Congratulations! It also s-says here that you're going to be lifted up by ropes or something so that it appears as if you're flying."

Great, Tootie thought, *I'm flying across the stage in front of gobs of people. Wearing what? My bathrobe?*

Suddenly Joey's expression changed and he pointed to the bottom of the card. "Read this," he said.

Tootie read: *I chose you because you are little and I did not want a big student to be lifted up by the ropes.*

Tootie's eyes narrowed, "I'm small, but I'm *not* little! I'm—oh, never mind." She didn't feel like explaining the difference between being small and being little. And besides, she felt absolutely sick about having to be center stage without the slightest inkling of what she was going to wear for a costume.

"Oh, Tootie, you'll be g-great," Joey said with a catch in his voice. "You're the biggest, greatest, stupendouest angel I know."

Tootie smiled warmly. Maybe Joey did understand after all.

Joey's face turned as red as a beet and then he continued stammering, "W-we'll s-show them. I'm going to make the best contraption this school has ever seen. And you're going to f-fly across the stage in front of everyone and s-s-say your lines for all to hear. And I'm going to shine the spotlight right on you."

"Just what I wanted," Tootie mumbled under her breath.

Miss Penick never did gain control again, and the moment the bell rang she dismissed the class.

"Come on, Joey," Tootie urged. "Let's get out of here. Even if there's snow on the ground, let's go play ball."

Joey nodded and opened his desk. "Don't forget to take home your mathematics book. We have a test tomorrow, and I-I'll help you study for it."

It wasn't long before they were in their coats and heading out the door. The bitter cold hit them in the face as they cautiously walked down the school steps. They looked around to find Pearl. She was standing by the fence with three of her friends, and she was sobbing.

"Now what!" Tootie said, exasperated. "Wait a few minutes, Joey."

Her feet slipped several times on the icy path as she hurried to her sister. "What's the matter?" Tootie gasped as she skidded into the group of girls.

Pearl pointed through the fence at the construction workers. There among the men was Banjo Ed!

"What!" Tootie shouted. "What's *he* doing here? I thought we'd never have to see him again."

"Shush!" Pearl demanded, and her pretty face looked pathetic. "My Eddie has come back."

"Oh, Pearl," Tootie pleaded.

"Be quiet," Pearl ordered. Her false front teeth moved up and down as she talked. "He hasn't even seen me. He's so busy digging that hole he hasn't looked up." Then Pearl turned to her friends. "Isn't he just the handsomest man you've ever laid eyes on? He's twenty-five!"

The girls stared at Banjo Ed with his black hair curling out from under his hard hat and his jacket stretching tight across his broad chest.

"Wow!" one of the girls exclaimed, "he *is* handsome!"

"He sure is!" another girl agreed. And then she turned to Pearl. "Isn't he the same one you were with at those street meetings?"

Pearl nodded ever so slightly.

Tootie felt sick. She couldn't believe Pearl was starting this kind of talk again after Mr. Harris had warned them to hush the gossip.

"I remember him," another girl spoke up. "He's the one who scared everybody with those stories about hell. And then he promised people they wouldn't go there if they gave him money. My parents thought it was a real scandal. In fact, they couldn't believe you were involved."

Pearl looked embarrassed.

Tootie kept her head lowered.

"It was stupid of me," Pearl admitted.

Everyone remained quiet, as if they were waiting for more explanation.

"I had my reasons." Pearl's voice sounded defensive

and she abruptly wiped her tears. "But look, Banjo Ed has another job." She pointed to the construction workers.

"Come on, Pearl, let's go home," Tootie suggested.

"No, not until I get a chance to talk with him."

"Please," Tootie pleaded. "He's working. You don't want to cause him trouble, do you?"

Just then Banjo Ed looked their way. He made a disgusted face and turned around and whispered something to one of his co-workers. The man laughed heartily and then they went back to their digging.

Pearl gasped. "Oh . . . I . . . think I'm going to die!" Then she began crying hysterically.

Tootie couldn't stand any more. She turned and hurried over to Joey who was waiting under a nearby tree. "I never want to be fifteen!" Tootie's curls shook as she stamped her feet. "Something happens to your brain when you turn fifteen."

Joey laughed. "Nothing's g-going to happen to you, Tootie McCarthy. You have too much c-common sense."

She tried her best to smile in spite of her tangled emotions. "Let's go get Buddy and play ball."

Before long, Tootie, Joey, and Buddy were all heading away from Washington Street toward the outskirts of town while tossing a tattered softball back and forth with their gloved hands. It had stopped snowing and the wind had died down but the air was crisp and cold, and they could see their breath as they talked.

Earlier that day, Mother had rummaged through

some boxes in the bakery basement and found two pair of old rubber boots. She insisted that Tootie and Buddy wear them to the open field. Tootie's were about three sizes too big and they made crunching sounds in the snow as she walked, but Buddy's boots fit perfectly. He was marching along as proud as could be.

As they turned the corner to the abandoned field, Joey slowed to pitch the ball to Buddy. Tootie ran ahead, but the moment she looked up, she saw the circle of brightly colored caravans. "Gypsies!" she screamed. "The Gypsies are here!"

"Wh-wh-what should we do?" Joey gasped.

"Quick! Let's hide over there." Tootie pointed to a clump of snow-covered bushes to the side of the abandoned lot, and she and Joey scampered over to them as fast as they could. Buddy didn't seem to understand the danger of Gypsies, and he stopped to look at the bright colors of the camp.

"Buddy McCarthy!" Tootie half-whispered in a panic. "Get over here. Right now!"

Buddy walked stubbornly to the bushes. He plopped down and began kicking at the snow mumbling, "Catch . . . catch . . . catch."

"We can't play," Tootie tried to explain. "The Gypsies are here!" Her voice quivered in fear, but she stretched up to get a better view. They were only about fifty yards away.

Buddy didn't understand what was going on and just yelled even louder, "Catch!"

"Hush, Buddy," Joey whispered. Scrambling onto

his knees, he leaned forward to take a closer look with Tootie.

They saw eight huge box-like wooden caravans arranged in a circle. Each looked like a house on wheels. The caravans were painted in reds, blues, and bright greens. Ornate wooden carvings hung above and alongside the front entrances, and they could see lace curtains at the side window of each caravan.

"I love their houses," Tootie whispered. "Don't you wish we could peek inside?" And then she gasped, "Oh, look!"

"Quiet!" Joey said again, but he too stared at the group of men coming out from behind one of the caravans. There were at least a half dozen of them, handsome, rugged, and each with a shock of long hair and a round earring in one ear. They wore dark jackets with big silver buttons and leather boots which came up to their knees. Trying to get everything tied down and secured for the night, they were hurrying around the campsite.

Two women wrapped in huge, colored shawls came out of one of the caravans and stood on the top step of the portable wooden platform. They hollered something to several women who were beginning to light a bonfire in the center of the circle of caravans. A number of children held their hands over the small licking flame, trying to gather some warmth.

A spicy odor filled the air and made Tootie's stomach growl with hunger. She had no idea what kind of food was being prepared, but it smelled delicious.

Buddy pointed excitedly to the edge of the field and a group of horses. Two men were removing harnesses. Bells, attached to the fancy harnesses, rang joyfully as the men worked. A teenage boy began covering the tethered horses with blankets, and he started singing a strange song as he rubbed and patted the animals.

> I'm the Romani rai
> I'm a true didikai
> I build all my castles beneath the blue sky,
> I live in a tent, and I don't pay no rent,
> And that's why they call me—the Romani rai

Joey whispered, "It l-looks like those horses were hitched to the c-caravans. Wh-what do you think?"

Tootie didn't answer. She was listening to the boy's song as he sang it over and over and, also, to the plaintive melody of a violin coming from inside one of the caravans. The sad, lonely tune floated across the camp and for some reason it brought tears to her eyes. She tried to wipe them away with her icy gloves.

Long minutes passed and the threesome continued in their hiding place, watching and listening. The leaping flames from the bonfire began to settle and caused sparkles to dance across the snow. The sun was getting low in the sky, and the entire scene looked like it had been painted with a gold-colored brush.

Suddenly Tootie noticed a girl, who looked about twelve or thirteen, walking their way. Her skin was a warm, copper color. Her features were delicate with a small straight nose, perfectly sculptured lips and beautiful black eyes.

Tootie nervously grabbed for Buddy and discovered he'd moved and was no longer hidden by the bush. Tootie pulled him back to her side.

Just then a woman by the fire shouted, "Mara!"

The girl stopped, turned, and said something to the woman. Tootie and Joey couldn't understand a word she said because she spoke in a fast, odd-sounding language.

Then the girl turned back toward them and smiled. She walked a little closer and said, "Hello."

Tootie was so scared she thought she would faint. She pushed Buddy into the snow for protection.

Suddenly the teenage boy who had been singing the song yelled something to the Gypsy girl. Mara turned and yelled, "Leon, they same age as we!"

Then she turned back to the frightened threesome and said, "Come." She looked directly at Tootie and then at Joey, and finally she stared at Buddy. Stretching out her hand, she invited again, "Come!" There was a lively lilt to her voice, but Tootie didn't trust her.

This is a trick to get us into their camp, Tootie thought frantically. Quickly she jumped up and grabbed Buddy's hand. Joey grabbed his other hand, and they started running through the snow, away from the Gypsies. They were practically carrying Buddy along as they trudged through the drifting snow. Tootie stumbled several times in her too-big boots but she clung desperately to Buddy.

When they finally reached Washington Street, Tootie

stopped and doubled over, trying to catch her breath. Buddy gasped and wheezed, and Joey didn't sound much better. A trolley bus jangled by, taking its load of passengers to their homes for the evening. Cars passed and several pedestrians hurried on their way. Everything seemed as before. It was as if no one even knew the Gypsies had arrived.

Tootie sputtered, "We made it!"

"Th-th-that was close," Joey stammered between gasps.

Buddy began crying. Tootie put her arm around him and immediately noticed that he had wet his pants. *It's no wonder!* she thought.

The moment she and Buddy entered the apartment she was bursting to tell about the Gypsies, but first she had to help Buddy change his clothes. As they went into the bedroom, she saw Pearl in bed with the blanket pulled over her head, sobbing. Tootie could hear the muffled sound of Pearl's voice: "Big Eddie! Oh, Eddie! Big Eddie!"

Just as Tootie was starting to comfort her, Mother called for help in the kitchen and Tootie hurried to set the table. She decided the subject of the Gypsies would have to wait.

About a half hour later, she pulled her chair next to Buddy's at the supper table. Pearl sat directly across from them, and Tootie noticed she still looked sad and her face was blotchy from crying. Mother sat at the far end next to Buddy, and Father presided at the head.

"Before I serve this delicious meal," Father paused and looked slowly around the table, letting his gaze settle briefly on each member of his family. Tootie held her breath, savoring the moment his full attention rested on her. Finally Father looked at Mother and continued, "Please, will you give thanks, Evelyn McCarthy?"

"Certainly, Donald," Eve replied, and the entire family bowed their heads.

Tootie never could recall a time when her father had offered thanks for the meal. He always said he would leave the praying and churchgoing to his wife. Nevertheless, Tootie felt grateful Father encouraged family prayer, especially tonight.

Mother's prayer was long. She gave thanks to God for the number of pies sold that day, the strength to keep working in spite of Mrs. Roseen's absence, and especially for God's hand of protection over her family. Finally Mother ended by saying, "And help us not to judge one another. Please help us to be kind to strangers, especially those who are different from us."

I wonder if that includes Gypsies, Tootie thought.

As soon as Mother breathed, "Amen," Father began serving the meal. The china plates were stacked in front of him, and he meticulously spooned mashed potatoes onto the first plate and topped them with creamed corn. Then he passed the plate to Mother and began serving Pearl's.

Tootie liked it that even though they were getting poorer by the day, her parents insisted on serving supper with style. She adored watching Father serve the meal on their fine china with a starched Irish linen tablecloth underneath. She did not feel so poor at supper time.

After everyone was served, Tootie glanced at Father in his black, pin-striped, three-piece suit, and watched as he carefully unfolded his napkin and placed it neatly in his lap. He waited, along with the rest of the family, for Mother to take the first bite before he began to eat.

Tootie was eager to tell them about the Gypsies, but she didn't know how to begin. Besides, her parents often scolded her when she talked at the table, saying, "Children are to be seen and not heard."

Finally Buddy blurted out, with mashed potatoes and corn squishing in his mouth, "Gyps . . . Gyps." He looked excited and his squinty eyes reflected pure joy. Tootie knew that he was trying to say Gypsies, but it was obvious no one else could understand.

"Hush," Father said. "Do not talk with food in your mouth."

"Gyps . . . Gyps," Buddy said again, after he'd swallowed his mouthful of dinner.

Reaching over, Mother wiped Buddy's chin. Then she moved his spoon in his hand to show him again how to hold it. Finally she took his spoon away and served him the next mouthful.

"Now, Eve," Father admonished, "how can the boy learn to eat properly if you're always doing it for him?"

Mother looked at Father quickly, but she put the spoon back into Buddy's hand.

Immediately Buddy bounced up and down on his chair and said, "Gyps . . . Gyps . . . nice!"

"What in the world?" father said with a frown. "Pearl, do you know what your brother's trying to say?"

"No," Pearl answered with her head still lowered. "I don't feel well, Daddy. Can I go to bed?"

Mother patted Pearl's hand. "You need to eat, dear, to keep your strength up."

Father turned to Tootie. "Well, Tootie, do you have any idea what Buddy's trying to tell us? He's certainly excited. Did something happen on your walk?"

This was not the way Tootie wanted to tell the news. And why in the world was Buddy saying the Gypsies were nice?

"Tootie," Father said with a slightly raised voice. "Quit your dillydallying and tell us what's going on!"

Tootie let the whole story come rolling out. She told about hiding behind the snow-laden bushes. She described her shock at seeing a circle of brightly colored Gypsy caravans in the middle of the old abandoned field when she, Buddy, and Joey went to play ball. She went on to tell how the Gypsies were dressed and about the horses, the boy's singing, and the lonely sound of the violin. She was so engrossed in her story that she tried to duplicate the sound of the violin by whining in a high squeaky pitch. Buddy did the same.

"That's enough, you two," Mother said with a smile. "We get the point."

Pearl roused herself from her depression long enough to comment, "I like the violin."

"Were you close enough to hear them talk?" Father asked.

"Yes," Tootie answered excitedly, "but we couldn't understand everything. They speak some English but they also speak another language." She repeated what she could remember about the boy's song. Then she told them about Mara. "There was this pretty Gypsy girl who saw us hiding and she started coming toward us. She could speak a little English because she said, 'Hello.'"

"Gracious, child," Mother exclaimed. "I've always told you to run from the Gypsies. We even talked about it again this morning. What in the world were you thinking about, Tootie? You certainly put yourself and Buddy in harm's way."

"Now, now, Eve. It sounds to me like the Gypsies were simply minding their own business and trying to prepare for the night. Imagine," Father continued, "just imagine what it must be like on a night like this inside one of those caravans."

Tootie tried her best to imagine. She could hear the wind and snow blowing against the door and windows of their apartment. What must it be like in one of those wooden caravans on wheels? She thought of Mara and Leon and wondered what they were doing. She remembered seeing small shutters on the side window of the caravans, and she pictured them shut against the bitter night.

Buddy bounced again and said, "Gyps . . . Gyps . . . nice."

"Why does he keep saying they were nice?" Mother asked, perplexed.

"Well, . . ." Tootie pondered. "Remember that Gypsy girl, Mara, that I told you about? Well, she invited us to come to their camp. I thought for sure she was tricking us."

Father leaned back in his chair. "And it seems obvious that our Buddy got the opposite impression; he believed she was being nice. Now, isn't this something to contemplate. Buddy often has unusual insight into people's true character. Maybe this Gypsy girl really was trying to be kind."

Mother gasped, "Oh, Donald, for pity sake! She was probably trying to lure our children into their camp, just as Tootie suspected."

Father dabbed the corners of his mouth with his linen napkin. "Come now, Eve, that sounds judgmental to me. What if everyone expected us to act a certain way simply because we're Irish? We wouldn't appreciate that at all, now would we? People seem to have this awful tendency to make false judgments about others, especially if they're different."

"Mama," Tootie said, "it's just like you said in your prayer."

"What?" Eve asked and frowned down the table at Tootie. "What did I say?"

"Well, you prayed just a few minutes ago that we'd be kind to strangers, even if they're different than us."

Mother sighed audibly. "That doesn't include Gypsies," she said.

Everyone stared at her.

Sheepishly, Mother defended, “Well, . . . I certainly wasn’t thinking about Gypsies when I prayed that.”

Father smiled and leaned forward to take another bite of his dinner. He chewed slowly and then commented, “This has certainly been a most delightful conversation. It’s been years since we’ve had a meaningful discussion around our table. Maybe it’s time we started allowing the children to speak while we have supper.” He stopped and looked at Eve.

Mother nodded. “They are growing up,” she admitted reluctantly. “But I still don’t think—”

“Oh, how I enjoy dinner talk,” Father interrupted. “It reminds me of the dinner parties we used to give when we were wealthy. Remember, Eve?”

“Yes, dear, I remember,” Mother said. The frown lines between her eyes softened and even the anxious look in her deep-set eyes seemed to ease. Then she said with a sigh, “Those were wonderful days, Donald, simply wonderful!”

The conversation shifted to an earlier era, but Tootie couldn’t get her mind off the Gypsies. Was the girl, Mara, really trying to reach out to them, or was it all a trick? Are the Gypsies bad people, or are they just different?

Tootie had no answers, but in her heart she determined to discover the truth.

Early the next morning, Joey hurried across Washington Street so he could walk the four blocks to Logan School with Tootie and Pearl. Cars crept slowly by and some swerved on the icy roads.

"Sorry I couldn't come over last night to work on our mathematics assignment." Joey puffed and sputtered as he reached Tootie's side. His breath hung like little clouds of fog in front of his face as he spoke.

"Don't worry about it," Tootie responded. She pulled up the collar of her coat against the cold wind. "Did you tell your folks about seeing the Gypsies?"

"No." Joey kicked at the snow. "I didn't want to get in trouble. What about you?"

Tootie glanced quickly at Pearl who was following a few steps behind. She appeared totally preoccupied by things other than Gypsies as she trudged along. Tootie turned back to Joey and whispered, "The whole story came out while we were eating supper."

"W-were your folks mad?" Joey asked.

Tootie didn't know how to answer. "Well," she said,

"I wouldn't exactly say they were mad. We had this long talk and I could tell Mama was really upset. Anyway, Daddy sort of took the side of the Gypsies."

Joey almost stumbled into a mound of snow. "What?" he gasped in surprise. "What do you mean? How can anybody defend G-G-Gypsies when they s-steal everything they get their hands on! They can't be trusted, Tootie. We know that for s-sure!"

"How? Just how in the world do we know that?"

Joey looked at her as if she had gone crazy. "*How?* You saw them. They l-looked awful with that long black hair and—and their f-funny houses and those stupid-looking clothes. And don't forget that girl with those black, b-beady eyes! She was trying to trick us. You know that, don't you?"

Tootie didn't answer right away. She kept walking. Finally she yanked her collar even higher to keep out the cold air and said, "No, Joey Staddler, I do *not* know that for sure and neither do you. Maybe Mara—and she didn't have beady eyes—was just trying to be kind and friendly."

Joey's mouth dropped open.

Tootie continued, "As a matter of fact, neither one of us knows for sure *what* she was going to do. But I'll tell you one thing, I'm going to find out the truth about those Gypsies."

Joey began to snicker, "Wow, you had me f-fooled for a while there. I was b-beginning to think you might be s-serious."

Tootie stopped dead in her big boots and stared at him. Pearl passed them without a word.

Joey leaned his head back and laughed. Flakes of snow landed on his upturned face and a few fell into his mouth. "Anybody who thinks the G-Gypsies are kind and friendly would have to be plumb loco!" He laughed again and the sound grated on Tootie's already taut nerves.

She fumed inwardly as she stood ramrod straight beside Washington Street, staring at her friend.

Joey didn't seem to notice. "I almost b-believed you were taking the side of the G-Gypsies and coming up with another one of your harebrained ideas."

"Sometimes, Joey Staddler, you make me spitting mad!" Tootie shouted. She hiked up her leggings, turned abruptly, and headed down the shoveled pathway after Pearl.

"Now wh-what's the matter?" Joey shouted after her. "What did I do? Girls! I'll never understand them!"

From the moment they reached the school grounds they heard gossip about the Gypsies. Even in the classrooms the teachers were warning the students to keep their distance from the Gypsy camp.

During lunch, Mr. Harris stood up on the stage at the far end of the large room. The lunch room was also the school auditorium and the gymnasium. But at noon every school day the tables and benches were arranged so all the students could eat together. Mr. Harris raised his hands indicating he wanted everyone to be quiet. The students were already orderly because the lunch room was always patrolled by several teachers. Mr. Harris announced with great agitation, "I want all of my Logan School students to be extremely cautious. I understand there are at least twenty Gypsy caravans parked not far from here and that they have brought enough animals with them to fill a circus."

Tootie was sitting next to Joey at one of the tables. She whispered, "Twenty, my eye! There were only eight caravans."

"And the only animals I s-saw were the horses," Joey whispered back with a frown. "I d-d-didn't even see any dogs. Did you?"

Tootie pursed her thin lips and her light brown curls bobbed back and forth as she shook her head. Her feelings were all mixed up. For some odd reason she felt like defending the Gypsies against the entire school.

The principal's eyebrows shot halfway up his forehead as he announced with a smug, almost prideful attitude, "We have too many important things on which to concentrate to waste our time and energy on the Gypsies. Our schoolwork is of utmost importance."

Several teachers nodded in obvious agreement.

"Then there's the Christmas play which will involve a number of practices," Mr. Harris continued. "And don't forget we're trying to do all this with that confounded construction going on right next door to our school." He irritably shook his bald head. "Now, let's not hear any further talk about that group of wandering Gypsies who don't have enough common sense to come in out of the cold."

Later that afternoon in mathematics class, Miss Penick stood behind her straight-backed chair with the ruler in one hand and the other flying through the air as she talked. “We have decided that our exam should be given orally. We believe this is a good indication of how we work under pressure and also an excellent measure of how we are progressing.”

Tootie’s stomach turned upside down. She hadn’t studied much lately, and this whole section on word problems was terribly confusing.

Miss Penick cleared her throat and continued, “Irene, we will give the first question to you.”

Tootie noticed that Irene looked smug as she quickly got out scratch paper and pencil.

“Ready?” Miss Penick asked.

“Yes, ma’am,” Irene said with confidence.

Miss Penick read from a mimeographed piece of paper: “Bill has four times as many quarters as dimes. In all he has $2.20. How many coins of each type does he have?”

Irene scribbled some figures on her paper and quickly spouted out: “Eight quarters and two dimes.”

“Correct,” Miss Penick said proudly. “We feel it is important that we learn how to solve these kinds of problems, especially since the Gypsies have come. They will try to cheat every store owner in town. Mark my word!”

Tootie frowned and quickly glanced over her shoulder at Joey.

He shrugged uncomfortably.

"Joey Staddler," Miss Penick announced. "We've all heard how Gypsies make paper flowers and then try to sell them to the public. Now, pretend with me that you were going to buy some of their homemade flowers to put in your parents' store. Let's say that the Gypsies wanted to sell you a dozen paper roses at $3.50 per dozen and bright carnations at $2.50 per dozen. In all, the Gypsies sold you 14 dozen, and the receipts totaled $43. How many dozen of each kind of paper flowers did the Gypsies sell you?"

Joey fidgeted with his pencil. He couldn't concentrate. Tootie huffed in disgust.

Miss Penick moved from her chair and came to stand by Joey. Her long nose with its coarse hairs seemed to hang over him. "Come on, young man," she tapped her foot as she spoke. "You are one of my prize pupils and we wouldn't want you to be cheated by those awful Gypsies over some silly paper flowers, would we?"

"Good gracious no!" Tootie exploded. "We certainly wouldn't want *that*!"

Miss Penick looked stunned and several students giggled.

Quickly Miss Penick turned on Tootie, "Why, the audacity of talking in such a manner! Outrageous! We will have none of that, Miss McCarthy. You Irish folks are entirely too hot-tempered and opinionated for your own good. Maybe it would serve you right if you went and lived with those Gypsies for a while."

"Maybe I could learn how to make paper flowers," Tootie mumbled under her breath.

"Speak up, young lady. We cannot hear you."

"Nothing, Miss Penick. I was just remembering how Mr. Harris told us not to keep talking about the Gypsies. That's all."

Miss Penick appeared flustered as she tried explaining that she wasn't exactly talking about Gypsies, but was simply using them as an example in the word problem.

Just then the bell rang and Miss Penick immediately dismissed the class.

Gypsies were the main topic for the next two days. Everyone had complaints against the Gypsies. Stories got bigger and more dramatic as they were told and retold at school, in the streets, and even in the McCarthy's Specialty Pie Bakery. Father wouldn't entertain the gossip, but it was there nonetheless.

Many times Tootie thought of going to the Gypsy camp, but deep inside she felt scared. The longer she put it off, the more nervous she became. Besides, Buddy had come down with the sniffles, and Mother always had plenty of work for her to do after school. To complicate matters, Pearl's old boyfriend, Banjo Ed, continued snubbing Pearl and she was more and more upset. Tootie knew in her heart that she should go and find the truth about Mara and Leon and the rest of the Gypsies. But it was easier to do nothing.

The days seemed to drag by, but finally Sunday morning arrived. Tootie began helping Buddy dress for church. "I'm glad you're feeling better," she said as she buttoned his flannel shirt.

Buddy grinned.

"Maybe we can go outside this afternoon. Would you like that?"

Buddy grinned even broader. "Catch," he said and clapped his hands. "Gyps . . . Gyps!"

At first she felt shocked that Buddy had remembered the Gypsies, but then she recalled all the gossip he'd heard throughout the week. "No, Buddy Boy, I'm not taking you to see the Gypsies."

Buddy shook his head and pouted.

Tootie finished buttoning his shirt. Buddy had lost his belt months earlier and they couldn't afford another one. Mama simply replaced it with a thin piece of rope which Tootie began to tie around Buddy's waist to hold up his brown corduroy knickerbockers. She pulled his wool socks up as high as they would go so that they fit under his knee-high pants. "There," Tootie said, trying to get his mind off the Gypsies, "now you don't have any skin showing. You should be warm enough on our walk to church." She pulled the legs of his knickerbockers to the sides to make them stand out all puffy.

Buddy giggled and put his small round head to one side. He grinned lovingly at Tootie and began to rock his thick body back and forth.

Tootie helped him into his coat and pulled down the flaps of his hat over his ears. She glanced sideways at Father who was already sitting in his favorite overstuffed chair and reading the newspaper. She knew he would read *The Tribune* from front to back and there would be plenty of talk about politics and the economy around the dinner table. She longed to have him join them for the church service because she felt confident he would like the preaching of their new pastor.

Oh, well, she thought, *Christmas is coming and Father will come to church on Christmas day.* Then she remembered the play at school and quickly tied her red wool scarf under her chin as she tried to shove away the disturbing fact that she still did not have any idea what she would wear for a costume.

Tootie, Buddy, Mother, and Pearl entered the Alliance Bible Church, hurried to the row where they usually sat, and slipped into the seat. Joey slid over next to Tootie. His parents sat in the row just ahead next to a woman with a fox fur collar. Tootie wondered how anyone could possibly want to wear such a thing.

After the congregational singing, the new young pastor got up and stood behind the pulpit. He looked troubled as he opened his big black Bible and announced he was reading from the second chapter of James.

> For if there come unto your assembly a man with a gold ring, in fine apparel, and there come in also a poor man in vile raiment, and ye have respect to him that weareth the fine clothing, and say unto him, sit thou here in a good place; and say to the poor, stand thou there, or sit here under my footstool, are ye not then partial in yourselves, and are become judges with evil thoughts?

Pastor Myers stopped and stared around at his congregation. His handsome face looked strained, and he paused for a minute, as if he were thinking what to say. Finally he proceeded, "Dear friends, I know I'm new here and I certainly don't want to begin by offending. But let me try to put this passage into perspective."

Again he paused, and this time it appeared as if he were silently praying. People became restless.

Pastor Myers continued, "Let's say, for instance, that a Gypsy came into our church building this morning. Would you hurry and seat the Gypsy here in the front? Would you seat him to the side? Or would you show him to the back pew?"

"I'd shove him right out the door," one of the parishioners said and chuckled.

There was stony silence as Pastor Myers tried to regain his composure. "I don't know who said that—for which I'm glad. Because that's the very attitude which concerns me. It concerns me deeply. I've talked with many of you this week, and instead of finding Christians who are reaching out to those who are different—like the Gypsies—I'm discovering that most are pulling away in fear and superstition."

Angry whispers erupted all across the congregation.

"Honestly," Pastor Myers continued, "how many of us here this morning have made it our duty to go out to the Gypsy camp and get to know them? Maybe they need help during this cold weather."

People began moving uncomfortably in their pews, and the lady with the fox fur collar jerked it so roughly that it appeared as if the fur were strangling her. Several people in the back row got up and walked noisily out of the service.

"How are we showing the love of Jesus Christ?" Pastor Myers asked undaunted. "Is Christ's love being demonstrated in practical ways through us as a church body?"

Tootie didn't understand what Pastor Myers meant by a church body, but she knew she was guilty of not showing Jesus' love. She hadn't given the Gypsies a chance, and she knew she had used her busy schedule, Buddy's cold, and even the weather as an excuse. Immediately she decided what she was going to do, even if she had to do it alone.

Joey nudged her.

Tootie looked up with tears shining in her eyes.

"I'll go with you," Joey mouthed silently.

She nodded and then they both concentrated on Pastor Myer's sermon, as if every word were necessary for their plan.

About an hour later the McCarthys were seated around the Sunday table. Father did all the talking. He shared one piece of information after another from the newspaper. Finally he began relating in great detail an article concerning President Calvin Coolidge and his wife Grace.

"Eve, don't you have any comment to make about your favorite first lady?" Father asked as he noted his wife's quietness.

"Excuse me, Donald?"

Father chuckled, "You're certainly deep in thought this afternoon. That new minister must've presented a mighty good sermon."

Eve looked surprised and then glanced at the children.

Pearl continued staring at her plate, as she had done during the entire meal. Tootie noticed she'd only eaten a few bites of Irish stew and was dejectedly pushing a piece of turnip back and forth across her plate with her fork.

Meanwhile, Buddy was thoroughly enjoying his stew

and had bits of vegetables and lamb around his mouth, with gravy dripping off his chin.

Father turned to Tootie, "Well, Tootie, I realize you are not usually allowed to talk at the table, but, seeing that everyone else is so preoccupied . . ."

Tootie moved uncomfortably. The last thing she wanted to do was to let her parents know that she and Joey were going to the Gypsy camp that afternoon.

But to Tootie's surprise, Father leaned toward her and completely changed the subject. "Tell me, how is your schoolwork going?"

"Fine," Tootie answered.

"And your mathematics? Any more difficulties brewing in that direction?"

Tootie shook her head.

"Did I hear something about a Christmas play that's being planned? Mrs. Peterson mentioned it earlier this week when she came into the bakery with Irene."

Tootie sighed audibly. "Yes, Father, there's going to be a play on Friday night. We've already started practicing."

"Well, listen to that, Eve. Christmas already. It seems just like yesterday that—"

Mother interrupted. "I hope you and Pearl are both in the choir this year. There's absolutely no money for any fancy costumes if you get parts in the actual play."

"Now, now," Donald chided in his happy-go-lucky manner. But he never stopped to find out if either of his daughters had been given parts or needed a costume.

Mother looked irritated. The dark circles under her eyes looked even darker as she responded, "Donald, it's easy to say 'Now, now, don't worry,' but it's a whole lot harder finding the money to make one of those costumes."

Tootie shifted miserably in her chair. Pearl just kept pushing the turnip around while Buddy slurped more gravy.

Eve continued, "There's always such a ridiculously competitive spirit at that school and everybody always tries to outdo last year's nativity dress. Even the props get more elaborate each year. Gracious! Where will all this end?"

Father shrugged in a disinterested way.

"It seems to me," Mother continued, "that the teachers are missing the whole spirit of Christmas by concentrating on such things. I've never understood why the costumes can't be stored and then simply reused. Doesn't that make a lot more sense?"

"Yes, dear," Donald said and leaned back in his chair as if to put an end to the subject.

Tootie thought her mother's idea about reusing costumes was great. She was about to say something when Father shoved his chair back slightly. He delicately dabbed the corners of his mouth with his linen napkin, then folded it and placed it alongside his plate. "Now that I have your attention, Eve, I want to tell you about an article I read concerning our economy. Maybe we'll get lucky. Maybe it's not too late for our pie business to start improving," he said hopefully. "This country's in for some good times ahead and there's no reason at all why we can't be a part of it."

As Father began explaining the article in his optimistic manner, Tootie's hopes sank. She was just about to tell them she needed an angel costume—immediately! And the last thing she wanted to hear was some highfalutin article on the country's economy. She hated this kind of talk because Father always got his hopes up that somehow their pie business would magically improve. But his hopes, along with the rest of the family's, always got dashed. In fact, each day they kept getting poorer and poorer.

Besides, Tootie thought rebelliously, *my problem about a costume is more important than the economy of this entire country!* She knew she had to put the angel outfit out of her mind for a little longer and try to concentrate on something else.

Right now I need to think of a plan for this afternoon and how I'm going to meet the Gypsies. No more hiding, she determined. *I'm going to walk right into their camp and say, "Hello." And then maybe I can help them do some work or something and maybe we can talk . . . or play ball . . . or ride horses. That's it! Maybe Mara and I can ride horses! And Joey can too, if he wants.*

Tootie kept dreaming during the remainder of the meal and even while she helped with the dishes.

After drying the last china plate, Tootie hurried to her room and put on her winter coat and tied her scarf firmly around her head. She was carrying her oversized boots in one hand as she quietly opened the bedroom door. Buddy was sitting on the floor in the living room as she tiptoed by. She felt fairly confident he hadn't seen her. But at the same time she also felt sort of bad because she'd promised to take him outside. But definitely not to the Gypsy camp! *Maybe I'll take him for a short walk when I get back,* Tootie reasoned.

Stealthily she opened the apartment door, put on her boots, and went down the outside stairs, holding onto the railing because the steps were slick.

"It's about t-time!" Joey complained as he stood at the bottom of the stairs, rubbing his gloved hands together. "I'm c-cold and I thought you'd never come."

"Sorry," Tootie said. "I couldn't get away any faster. Let's go." She turned and headed down the middle of the shoveled pathway, her feet making crunching sounds on the snow. Joey had a hard time keeping up.

"Hold it!" he hollered. "Wh-what's our plan?"

"We're going to walk right into their camp and say, 'Hello.'"

Joey halted. "You've got to be k-kidding!"

Tootie grabbed his arm and pulled him along. "I've thought this whole thing through," she explained. "I think we should just walk right up to them and introduce ourselves. Then maybe they'll invite us into their caravan. I really want to see inside. And then maybe we can ride their horses."

"Come on, Tootie. You m-must be joking. I'm s-sure they're not going to let us ride horses in weather like this. That'd be plumb s-stupid! And the last thing we should do is go inside one of those caravans. That's just asking for it!"

"Well," Tootie defended, "what do you suggest?"

Joey shrugged. "Let's watch them first—just to see if it's s-safe."

Tootie hedged, "I guess that'd be O.K. But just for a while. I'm not hiding like some scaredy-cat. That's for sure."

"I'm no scaredy cat," Joey defended. "I'm just thinking we should be careful!"

"They're not bad people," Tootie said with confidence. "I have this feeling that they're good, just like Pastor Myers said." And for the first time all week, she felt brave. It was a great feeling, and it added speed to her step. "We've misjudged them, Joey. I'm sure of it. In fact, we'll probably all become the best of friends."

Tootie visualized herself and Mara riding through the street side by side with the bells on the horses' reins ringing loudly. Joey just shook his head and mumbled, "Girls."

Finally Tootie and Joey headed away from Washington Street toward the field where the caravans were parked. As they got closer Joey whispered, "L-let's hurry across to those bushes. We can see from there."

Tootie agreed with some reservation. "But we're just looking. We're not hiding."

"Right," Joey agreed.

They ran as quickly and quietly as they could to the bushes and fell behind the large, snow-covered mound. They scrambled onto their knees and peered over the top. Tootie gasped for breath and so did Joey. To their utter surprise the Gypsies were setting up a huge pine tree in the middle of the circle of caravans. A blazing bonfire was burning nearby, and colorfully dressed Gypsies were milling about everywhere.

"Wh-what do you think they're doing?" Joey asked.

Tootie pointed to Mara who held a handful of gold and silver tinsel. Several other girls were by her side and they too had handfuls of the glittering stuff. "I guess they're going to decorate a Christmas tree," Tootie answered, trying her best to sound brave.

Just then a broad-shouldered man with an enormous belly came out of one of the caravans. His face was dark and weather-beaten, and he had a huge bushy mustache and heavy eyebrows. The rest of the Gypsies made way for him and one man showed him to a wooden bench close to the fire. He wore baggy trousers and a jacket adorned with silver buttons like all the other men, but the Gypsies revered him greatly. *It's his manner,* Tootie decided. *He acts like he's the boss.*

Then several women helped an old woman descend the same portable wooden steps in front of the caravan. The helpers hung onto the old woman as if she were fragile. She was wrapped warmly in bright shawls, and she too was led over to the fire and seated comfortably next to the man. Even from this distance, Tootie could see that the old woman's skin hung on her bones like limp lettuce. She lifted her hand and placed a long clay pipe between her lips.

Tootie gasped. She'd never seen a woman smoke a pipe.

And then, from out the same caravan came a second

woman, but she was very unlike the first. She wore huge dangling earrings and her bosom almost bulged out of her blouse. With great deliberation she rearranged her shawls warmly around her buxom figure and sat down by the fire on the other side of the man. She burst into laughter as the sounds of the violin floated across the cold air, and she clapped and motioned toward Mara.

Mara and the rest of the girls began singing and dancing as they adorned the pine tree with the gold and silver tinsel. They danced with little steps, moving slightly forward and sideways, completely encircling the tree. Their dainty hands moving, joining, and parting to place one piece of tinsel at a time on the tree. Their long, brightly colored skirts swung around their booted feet as they swayed back and forth in the snow.

They sang the same songs over and over in some odd-sounding language that Tootie and Joey did not understand.

Suddenly in all the drama of decorating the Christmas tree, a young boy darted into the circle. He was yelling with great delight and holding up an animal which he had obviously caught in a trap.

"It looks like a porcupine!" Tootie whispered hoarsely, not taking her eyes off the struggling animal.

"Wh-what do you think they're g-g-going to do with it?" Joey asked, breathlessly.

Just then the large man by the fire jumped to his feet, held his clenched fist high in the air and shouted, "A feast! A feast! A feast!"

All the Gypsies cheered.

Gooseflesh ran up and down Tootie's spine and her Irish stew came up into her throat. "They're going to eat it!" she whispered and swallowed several times, trying desperately to keep from throwing up. "Let's get out of here!"

Joey's voice came out in a high squeak, "If they eat p-p-porcupines, m-maybe they'll eat people!"

At that very moment Tootie and Joey heard a familiar cry. Tootie didn't believe her ears and shook her head several times. *It can't be,* she thought frantically.

But then, to her horror, she saw the Gypsy boy, Leon, coming into the camp leading Buddy by the hand. Buddy was crying hysterically. He looked cold and frightened. He wore only his flannel shirt and corduroy knickerbockers. He had no coat or hat.

Tootie forgot all fear and hot searing anger filled her whole body. *Nobody's going to eat my Buddy Boy!* She dashed out from behind the bush screaming, "Buddy! Buddy! Run!"

Tootie ran directly toward the Gypsy camp to rescue her brother. She grabbed frantically for his hand, almost pushing Leon into the side of one of the caravans.

Leon said haltingly, "We friends." He was taller than Tootie had expected, and younger. He smiled boyishly and said again, "We friends."

"Oh, sure!" Tootie screamed at him as she pulled Buddy to come with her.

In a panic, Joey ran forward and grabbed Buddy's other hand.

Buddy's crying had quieted some since he'd seen his sister, but he kept sobbing, "Toooootie . . . Toooootie . . . Toooootie."

The large man seated by the fire and the boy with the squirming porcupine began walking toward them. They were talking rapidly in some gibberish or foreign-sounding language.

Tootie and Joey stared at them for a brief second and then at each other. Fear shot wildly through their veins, and they turned in unison and began pulling Buddy along with them. They ran frantically through the snow, away from the Gypsy camp. Tootie thought she heard raised voices behind them, but she was too afraid to look back. *They might put a spell on us, grab us, and eat us.* On and on they ran. They ran the four blocks to Washington Street. As they turned the corner, they stumbled squarely into Pastor Myers.

"Hey," he yelled. "What's this?"

"Run!" Tootie screamed. "Run!"

Pastor Myers held his hands out in front of the wide-eyed threesome. "Slow up. What's going on?"

"The Gypsies are after us," Tootie gasped and turned to point down the street. No Gypsies were in sight. "I'm telling you, Pastor Myers, they were chasing us. They're going to eat us!"

"Eat you!" the Pastor repeated in astonishment. "Why, I've never heard such nonsense in all of my life." Shaking his head in disbelief, he looked directly at Tootie. "Come on, young lady, you know better than that!"

Joey interrupted. "They c-c-captured B-Buddy and they were going to eat him, just like they were doing with the p-p-porcupine."

"Inside," Pastor Myers said in a strained tone and nodded his head toward the church entrance. "You must calm down. Besides, you're wet and cold, especially this little brother of yours."

Tootie looked at Buddy and was shocked when she saw him shivering. Flakes of snow laced his hair and clothes. She scanned the streets once more through the early evening dusk to see if there were any Gypsies in sight, and then she darted up the church steps after the others.

Pastor Myers led them across the dimly lit foyer and down the narrow hallway to his office. Immediately he went into the adjoining bathroom and brought back a few towels. He began drying the snow off Buddy's hair while Tootie and Joey paced the room.

"Tell me what this is all about," Pastor Myers said. "You two can't go around shouting that the Gypsies are going to eat people. There's already too much gossip in this town. It's spreading like gangrene! Now, start from the beginning and tell me everything."

Tootie picked up another towel and began wiping Buddy's face, neck, and arms and dusting the snow off his knickerbockers and socks. "It's not just gossip, Pastor Myers." And she almost choked on her words. "I was ready to go into the Gypsy camp and make friends with them. Honest I was!"

"Me, too," Joey added.

Buddy sneezed and pulled away from Pastor Myers and Tootie.

"There, there now, Buddy Boy," Tootie soothed and pulled him gently into her arms, burying his head in the crook of her neck. "There, there, nothing's ever going to happen to you again. I'm here to protect you from those awful people, and so is Joey."

Joey stopped his pacing and said proudly, "Th-that's right, Buddy. You can depend on m-me!"

Pastor Myers flung the towel into Joey's hand, walked over to his desk, and sat down. He was there only a brief moment when he got up again and began pacing with great agitation.

Tootie and Joey frowned at each other and kept drying Buddy and then themselves. Tootie's breathing was almost back to normal when she removed her coat and put it around Buddy's shoulders.

Finally Pastor Myers went back to his desk and sat down again, sighing deeply. He put his elbows on the big green desk blotter and let his head rest dejectedly in his hands. "I thought that after you two left the church service this morning, you were going to be different from all the rest. For some reason I got the distinct impression that you two were really listening to my sermon."

"We were," Tootie admitted. "That's why we went to the Gypsy camp."

Joey agreed.

"Well, then, what happened?" Pastor Myers asked again. "Just tell me from the beginning. I don't understand any of this."

As Tootie and Joey began relating the whole incident, Buddy leaned against Tootie. She kept patting him as she told about hiding behind the bushes and watching the Gypsy girls dance while they decorated the Christmas tree.

Then Joey went on to tell about the boy who came running into the camp holding a captured porcupine. "And the huge Gypsy by the f-fire shouted, 'A feast! A feast!'" Joey said and shivered. "They were g-going to eat that poor animal!"

"That's right," Tootie added. "And then this Gypsy boy, Leon, came into the camp pulling Buddy by the hand. Buddy was screaming and crying. I'm sure they were going to eat him, too." Tootie's eyes were big and her wet curly bangs were matted down against her forehead.

"Now we're getting someplace," Pastor Myers said and rose to his feet. "You two simply jumped to the wrong conclusion. You see, when I was visiting at the Gypsy camp a couple of days ago they told me they were hoping to catch a porcupine. They told me that they're especially fond of the white meat. They even showed me how it was going to be cooked; in clay, in the fire. Anyway, they say it tastes sort of like chicken."

Tootie and Joey looked at each other and their lips curled up in disgust.

"Let's see, where was I," Pastor Myers continued. "Oh, it might help to know what that boy, Leon, said when he entered the camp with your brother. I know him. He's thirteen and he has a twin sister. They both speak a little English. Now, try to remember exactly what he said because I'm certain Leon was not intending to roast Buddy along with the porcupine."

Tootie looked at Joey and then back at the pastor. "Well, I guess he said something like, 'We friends.'"

Joey shook his head in agreement.

Buddy jumped up and down several times. "Friend

. . . friend," he repeated in his simple way. His thin hair, which had been towel-dried, was sticking straight up. Then Buddy nodded his small round head excitedly and said, "Gyps . . . Gyps."

Pastor Myers rushed over and grasped both Buddy's hands. Leaning over, he smiled intently right into Buddy's face. "Listen, young man, are you saying that the Gypsies are your friends?"

Buddy grinned and awkwardly shook his head, "Gyps . . . friend."

"Oh, blessed be God!" the pastor exclaimed. "From the mouth of babes! Finally! Finally someone in this town is without prejudice. Oh, Buddy McCarthy, you are an answer to my prayers!"

It felt as if a knot were cinched tight around Tootie's chest.

Joey stepped forward. "I don't think that's what Buddy's trying to say. He can't mean *that!* Those Gypsies aren't his friends."

Tootie turned Buddy around to face her. She held his shoulders and looked squarely into his face. She had to know the truth. "Were you trying to find me, Buddy Boy? Is that why you were out there? Were you lost?"

Tears filled his eyes. Slowly one tear escaped and trickled down his puffy face. Then he put his head back and cried toward the ceiling, "Toooootie! Toooootie! Toooootie!"

It all became clear. Tootie could imagine Buddy looking around the apartment and discovering his sister was gone—the sister who had promised to take him outside. She could see him running out of the apartment and down Washington Street without any coat or hat, frantically looking for her, calling her name. He had probably tried to get to the old abandoned field and that's when Leon found him. That Gypsy boy wasn't going to eat Buddy, he was saving him! Shame flooded her whole being.

"I'm sorry, Buddy Boy," Tootie said through her tears. "You must have had an awful fright when you couldn't find me. Didn't you?"

Buddy nodded his head.

Tootie swallowed hard and continued, "All I can say, Buddy, is that I'm sorry. I'm really, *really* sorry! I guess Joey and I sort of let our imaginations run away with us. I bet that scared you all the more."

"Hold it!" Joey said disgustedly. "You remember that poor p-p-porcupine, don't you? That wasn't just our imagination!"

"No," Tootie admitted. "That was a porcupine all right. And they did say they were going to eat it. And they probably will eat it just like Pastor Myers said. But that doesn't mean they were going to eat Buddy."

"Well . . ."

"It's understandable," Pastor Myers encouraged. "We all make mistakes and sometimes we jump to the wrong conclusions."

His gentle words were soothing.

"But what still concerns me," Pastor Myers continued, "is that this entire town is against those Gypsies. As I said, I've been out to their camp and I find them wonderful people. They're the first to admit that most Gypsies have a bad reputation, and they understand why. But they told me that they are different. They are a good decent group, or clan, or 'kumpama' as they would say. And I believe them."

Joey hit his fist against the palm of his hand. "I was so s-sure they were b-bad."

"Me, too," Tootie admitted.

Buddy looked around the circle at all the sad, worried faces. He began clapping his hands loudly and shouting, "Gyps . . . Gyps . . . nice!" Before he could stop himself, he sneezed, spraying everywhere. Then he grinned sheepishly and said, "Uh-oh."

Tootie looked at Pastor Myers, over at Joey, and then back at Buddy. Quickly she wiped her brother's face with her glove and then stuffed the messy glove in her pocket.

Buddy began to giggle and immediately everyone burst into laughter. It felt so good. The tension which had held them so firmly was gone, and even the taut muscles in Tootie's neck began to relax.

Pastor Myers smiled. "We needed something to help us through this heavy discussion. Seriously though, we owe a lot to this little brother of yours, Tootie. He may not be as bright in some ways as other boys his age, but God has given him a unique insight into people. In the midst of his own fear, he found a friend. I would definitely call Buddy McCarthy a very special child."

Tootie didn't know what to say. No one, outside of

her family, had ever spoken so kindly about her retarded brother.

Pastor Myers walked over to the coat rack. "I have this old jacket hanging here. Why don't you put it on, Tootie, seeing that you've already given yours to Buddy? This will help a little on your way home."

"Thanks," Tootie said. "I'll give it back tomorrow."

"No rush. You three had better get going before it turns any colder."

"And here," Joey said, "wear this." He plopped his hat on top of Buddy's head.

Tootie and Joey held Buddy's hands and smiled, first at him and then at each other. They knew they were leaving Pastor Myers' office somehow changed; somehow more grown-up.

Later that night as Tootie lay snuggled under the rough wool blankets, she thought back over the lessons she'd learned that day. She could hear Buddy's labored breathing coming from his side of the room as he restlessly thrashed back and forth in his bed. *I hope he doesn't catch his death of cold like Mama predicted,* Tootie thought.

And then she heard Pearl's soft whimper coming from her side of the bed. She was moaning something over and over.

Tootie listened. Between the raspy breathing of Buddy and the muffled sounds of her parents' discussion in the other room, Tootie couldn't quite make out what Pearl was saying. She reached over and brushed

Pearl's black straight hair away from her face and was about to speak to her when Pearl pulled away and scooted as far away from Tootie as she could get.

Tootie turned onto her side and bit her quivering lower lip. "I love you, family," she whispered softly into the night air. "Everything will be all right." She said it more to reassure herself than anything, but just saying it helped.

To her surprise, Pearl's whimpering stopped and Buddy began to sleep peacefully. *A few kind words really* do *help,* she thought.

Then she remembered Mara and her twin brother, Leon. She wished with all her heart that she had said a few kind words to them.

Tootie woke with a start. The first thing on her mind was that she needed her angel costume by two o'clock that afternoon. Dress rehearsals were to begin and Miss Penick had instructed everyone to bring their costumes so that she could see them.

Unexpectedly Buddy moaned, and Tootie jumped up and hurried to his bed. As she touched him, it felt to Tootie like he was burning up. She ran to the door, yelling, "Mama, Buddy's sick!"

Eve came into the room. "I know, Tootie. I've been checking him throughout the night. He's had a high fever for the past several hours, but I think it's beginning to come down."

Pearl slipped out of bed and hurried to the bathroom. She didn't even stop to look at Buddy.

"I'm sorry, Mama. I should have taken better care of him."

"None of that, Tootie," Eve said and brushed back a few strands of graying hair which had escaped from her quickly made bun. "You're not to blame. You had no idea whatsoever that Buddy had gone after you. Really, Tootie, in a way we're all to blame; he's the family's responsibility."

Tootie still felt guilty and her face must have showed it because Mother continued, "Cheer up, lass. It's not the end of the world. It's just a bad cold. You hurry and get ready for school while I tend to your brother."

Tootie looked anxiously down at Buddy and then at Mother with tears brimming in her huge hazel eyes. "Should I stay home and help?"

"No need," Mother said as she began fluffing and rearranging Buddy's pillows and straightening the covers. "Besides, he'll probably sleep most of the day. He's come through worse colds than this, but don't forget to pray for him."

"I won't, Mama. I won't forget."

Tootie leaned over and kissed her sleeping brother on his fevered forehead. "I love you, Buddy Boy. Please get better," she whispered gently.

On her way to school with Pearl, Tootie tried her best to concentrate on the day ahead. The morning air was crisp and cold and a fresh layer of snow covered everything. A few cars crept by and a trolley bus jangled slowly on its way. Tootie wanted to get Pearl to talk as they walked down the snow-covered boardwalk along Washington Street. She wanted to ask Pearl's advice about the angel costume, and she also wanted to tell Pearl about the Gypsies. But Pearl was more withdrawn than ever, and Tootie didn't know how to help her come out of her depression. She didn't even know what to say. She gave up trying when they reached the school grounds, and each went her own way.

Tootie saw Joey and they walked into the school building together. As they were heading down the hallway they came to the principal's office, which was overflowing with angry parents. She heard someone yell furiously, "We demand that those Gypsies be run out of town!"

Then a woman whose voice Tootie recognized from church complained, "I'm scared to death for my own children. What kind of influence will those people have on our kids?"

"I think those Gypsies are going around stealing animals," another voice accused. "My little boy's puppy is missing. And my husband says he thinks he's missing some *money.*"

"That's right!" everyone agreed. "Those Gypsies are a bunch of thieves!"

Mr. Harris tried his best to calm the mob. "Listen, everyone, I've already talked with the authorities about your concerns and, I might add, they are also my concerns. The Chief of Police has reassured me he's doing all he can to make those Gypsies leave town! He told me that the head Gypsy informed him they want to leave, and they'll do so as soon as the weather improves. They were on their way somewhere else when the snowstorm hit."

As Tootie and Joey watched, they saw the principal raise his eyebrows and nod his bald head toward Miss

Penick, who quickly began squeezing her way to the front of the crowd.

"Please—please everyone!" she said and waved her long, thin arms. "Let's keep calm. We have just been informed that the superintendent of schools is coming this Friday to see our Christmas performance. We'll try our level best to get those dreadful Gypsies to leave town by that date. We don't want any disturbance whatsoever in this school while Superintendent Henry is around."

"Superintendent Henry is coming this Friday?" one of the parents asked in dismay. "That's Friday the thirteenth!"

Another parent added anxiously, "Something's bound to happen on Friday the thirteenth with those Gypsies so close. They'll use this time to put some magic spell on us!"

The parents continued talking, but just then one of the adults shut the office door right in Tootie's and Joey's faces.

"This is awful!" Tootie gasped. "They sound like a lynching mob. What are we going to do?"

"Wh-what *can* we do?" Joey responded.

All day the gossip surrounding the Gypsies got bigger and bigger, mingled with fears of Friday the thirteenth and curses, spells, and witchcraft. Everyone's fears increased more and more as the day progressed.

At exactly two o'clock Miss Penick announced that play practice was about to begin and asked to inspect each costume.

Irene quickly bent over and pulled out a shopping bag from under her desk. From the bag she extracted the most beautiful blue robe and white flimsy shawl that Tootie had ever seen. "This is my costume for the part of Mary," Irene said proudly to the teacher. "My mother just threw it together in seconds."

"It's very pretty!" Miss Penick exclaimed. "Come up here, dear, and show the class. I'm sure it's prettier than last year's. Oh my, yes, it's much prettier!"

Irene pranced and pivoted in front of the class and held up her costume for all to see. Then she said coyly, "I've memorized my lines just perfect, Miss Penick. I won't make one mistake. Do you want to hear them?"

"In a few minutes," the teacher said and smiled broadly. "You're such a star pupil. We hope everyone else has come just as prepared as you." Then Miss Penick turned toward the class and Irene slowly walked back to her desk, grinning all the way.

"Take out your costumes and have them ready," Miss Penick announced. Then she started going from desk to desk on the other side of the room. Almost everyone had something to show. A few had samples of material and explained that the costume would be finished by tomorrow.

Joey poked Tootie in the back, "Do you have yours?" he whispered.

Tootie didn't turn around, but she shook her head back and forth.

"Wh-what are you going to say?" Joey asked.

Tootie shrugged. Outwardly she appeared calm, but

deep down she felt panicky. Her heart was pounding and her mouth was as dry as cotton wool. She didn't have a clue what she was going to say. How would it sound if she told the truth? *Sorry, Miss Penick, we're too poor. My parents can't afford an angel outfit. But my sister suggested I wear my old faded bathrobe. Would that do? No,* she decided, *I definitely can't say that.*

Oh, God, she started to pray. And then she quit. She felt disappointed and even a little mad at God because she'd prayed about an angel costume last week and he hadn't given her one. *I guess he just doesn't care about stuff like this,* she reasoned irritably.

As Miss Penick proceeded around the classroom, Tootie got more and more nervous. It was almost her turn, and she still didn't know what she was going to say. Soon Miss Penick was standing over her desk, looking down her long nose.

"Well, young lady, we want to see what you've brought."

Tootie didn't look up.

"We are waiting," Miss Penick said. "Hurry now, we already have a shortened practice time this afternoon."

Before Tootie could stop herself, she was telling the most fantastic lie to Miss Penick and to the entire class that she had ever told. "It's like this," Tootie began. Her eyes were big and dilated and she kept licking her lips with her dry tongue. "I have the most beautiful gorgeous white dress that anyone has ever seen. The white material is all shiny. It sort of shimmers. I think it might be silk or chiffon or something like that. Anyway, it simply flows all around me and it will be perfect for my part as the head angel."

Miss Penick gasped.

"And I've decided not to wear wings," Tootie continued, almost breathless. "I think they will take away from my whole outfit. Anyway, it will be more dramatic if I'm lifted high up into the air without any wings by this fantastic contraption that Joey's making."

"Yes, yes!" Miss Penick said with great enthusiasm. "I see what you mean!"

"Wow!" someone from the back of the classroom exclaimed. "This is going to be the best play ever!"

Tootie swallowed several times. "I also have this string of diamonds that I'm going to wear in my hair," she lied. "It sort of looks like a halo!"

Tootie almost believed it herself. It had been surprisingly easy. It was a whole lot easier than admitting the truth—at least, for the moment.

"This is simply marvelous!" Miss Penick said, and her arms literally flapped. "Bring everything with you tomorrow so that we can see them." Then she stopped and a frown creased her face. "But I admit that all this is quite surprising to me. For some reason we weren't expecting something so . . . so grandiose from you McCarthys."

Suddenly Tootie felt justified. *What nerve!*

Miss Penick turned to Joey, "Well, young man, this news is wonderful! Tell us about this fantastic contraption, as Tootie puts it. What's your idea? How are you going to lift Tootie off the stage and make it appear as if she's flying?"

Joey hedged. He hadn't come up with any idea. He'd thought and thought about how to lift Tootie, but he hadn't been able to figure it out. And now everybody thought he had some clever plan.

"Well," Miss Penick smiled, "we see that you are reluctant to give away your secret. But no more stalling, Joey Staddler. We're in a hurry."

Tootie didn't dare turn around and look at Joey. She knew he was fuming because he'd already kicked her under the desk.

Joey fiddled with his suspenders and let them snap back into place. Finally he said, "It's not n-nearly ready yet, Miss Penick. I have lots to do b-before it's ready."

"Gracious, boy, the performance is this Friday. You'd better get busy."

"Yes, ma'am," Joey said in a low tone.

"Well," Miss Penick continued, "have you fixed up the lights, or have you been dillydallying around about them too?"

Everyone knew the Staddlers were one of the first in the city to use spotlamps. They attached them inside the store windows at night. All the rest of Washington Street was lit by gas lamps.

"I've got the lights r-ready," Joey said defensively. "Here they are," and he pointed under his desk. "My dad is letting me use the b-big spotlamps we turn on at night to p-protect our place. We've put these reflectors on them."

Miss Penick nodded as if to interrupt. Then she turned around to the class and announced, "Tomorrow we're going to spend most of the day rehearsing. All lines must be memorized, so come prepared. We need to be ready because Superintendent Henry is coming Friday night for the performance."

Then she turned back to Joey. "Listen, young man, I want you to bring the rest of your equipment tomorrow without excuse. This is of utmost importance. How can we show off Tootie's angel costume if she isn't lifted high into the air? That's the grand finale!"

Tootie felt ashamed of herself for lying about her own costume and now she felt even worse because she'd gotten Joey in trouble. *What should I do?* But as soon as she asked herself, she knew the answer. She raised her hand.

Miss Penick ignored her and turned to the class. "This year's performance, costumes, and props must be better than last year's. We want to show everyone. And we want to impress Superintendent Henry. I think having an angel lifted high above the stage will be just the thing. It will be the grand finish."

Then Miss Penick turned and called on Tootie. For the moment she forgot all about her terrible lying and how she was about to confess.

"Excuse me," Tootie said, "but I think that the baby Jesus should be the grand finale, Miss Penick, don't you? After all, this *is* the Christmas play and *he* should be the center of attention."

"Yes . . . yes, of course!" Miss Penick defended. "But

Joey is bringing two spotlights. Remember? One will shine on you as you are lifted high above the stage. And the other one will shine on the cradle scene and the baby Jesus. Now, how does that sound, little Miss Uppity?"

"Fine, ma'am," Tootie said, embarrassed. She knew she deserved that rebuke. But she also knew she was going to get much more than a rebuke if she didn't come up with an angel costume—real soon!

As soon as the dismissal bell rang Joey whispered to Tootie, "Come on, l-let's get out of here!"

Tootie felt relieved that Joey was still talking to her after she'd told such awful lies. She was putting her schoolbooks away and gathering her homework assignments when Pearl came into their classroom. Tootie was surprised to see her.

Pearl's pale white skin looked almost gray and her black hair had lost some of its shine. She slouched slowly to Tootie's desk. Several students looked her way and a few began whispering. Tootie knew her sister had been depressed lately, but now the whole world could tell at one glance.

"Come on, Pearl, let's go home," Tootie said in an unnaturally cheerful voice. "Let's see how Buddy's doing."

Pearl looked straight ahead and said in a monotone, "I'm staying around here for a while." Her false front teeth slipped as she talked. But for once, she didn't even try to hide them.

"What's the matter?" Tootie asked, concerned. "Do you have to stay after school?"

Pearl didn't answer. Instead she turned and left the room just as dejected and forlorn as she had entered.

"Well," Tootie said, looking at Joey, "remind me never to turn fifteen!"

Tootie tried her best to shrug off the nagging feeling of responsibility toward her older sister, but she was becoming more concerned about Pearl by the day. Quickly she turned to Joey, "Come on, let's get out of here."

They rushed into their coats, and Tootie tied her red scarf tightly as Joey put on his hat. Soon they were out of the building and were just about to leave the school grounds when they heard Pastor Myers yelling at them from the church steps, kitty-corner from the school. He motioned for them to come and join him.

"Good afternoon," he greeted them as Tootie and Joey rushed to his side. "Thanks for coming over. It's cold, isn't it?"

"S-sure is," Joey agreed.

Pastor Myers rubbed his hands together and moved from one foot to the other, trying to get warm. "I just wanted to see you two and find out how you were doing after yesterday's ordeal."

"Oh, we're fine," Tootie offered and looked at Joey. They both knew that was far from the truth. She probably should have said that neither one of them was one bit fine because she needed an angel costume and Joey needed to discover some angel-lifting equipment by tomorrow. And then she probably should have told him about the changes in Pearl. Maybe he could help. But she left all of this unsaid. Finally she added, "Sorry I forgot to bring your jacket, Pastor Myers."

"Don't worry about that." He pulled the collar of his old coat even higher and turned his back against the cold wind. "It wouldn't be any help in weather like this. Anyway, I don't want to keep you two for long. I just wanted to tell you that I've been to your house, Tootie, to check on your brother."

Tootie's heart began to race. "Is he all right?"

"Well, he still has a high fever and he's certainly given your mama lots of worries. But Buddy's cold is no surprise after he caught such a chill."

"He's going to be O.K. . . . isn't he?" Tootie questioned again.

"I'm sure he will," Pastor Myers smiled. "We had a good time of prayer together."

Tootie breathed a sigh of relief, and so did Joey.

"But I also wanted to tell you," the Pastor continued, "that after I visited with your parents and prayed with Buddy, I walked over to the Gypsy camp. I happened to mention your brother to them, and they said that they would make some herb tea for him to help bring down his fever. I gather they all drink it quite often during the winter."

Tootie and Joey stared at the Pastor and then at each other. They couldn't believe he was talking about the Gypsies' offer of help so matter-of-factly.

Pastor Myers continued with a smile, "They also told

me that they would mix up some concoction to rub on Buddy's chest. I think it's for congestion. I got most of this information from Mara and Leon because the rest of them speak very little English. Anyway, will you pass that message on to your folks?"

"I sure will!" Tootie said, and her whole expression was one of surprise.

Pastor Myers chuckled. "Isn't this amazing? Those Gypsies want to help."

"B-b-but they don't even know Buddy," Joey added.

"I realize that. But they want to help nonetheless." Pastor Myers turned toward the church entrance. "I've been out visiting most of the day and I'm tired and cold. I'll be going home soon, if you will pass on the message for me."

Tootie nodded, almost dumbfounded.

"Much obliged," Paster Myers smiled.

She and Joey watched as their pastor headed up the church steps mumbling, "God works in mysterious ways."

They took one look at each other and knew instantly what they were going to do.

"We'd better hurry," Tootie said.

Joey agreed.

Before they had time to reconsider, Tootie and Joey ran through the snowy streets to the Gypsy camp. When they arrived everything looked the same as it had the day before: the tinseled Christmas tree and the brightly burning bonfire in the middle of the circle of caravans. Three women were standing by the fire near a cast-iron stewing pot. The smell of something hot and spicy filled the air. The women looked at the two young people with surprise.

"Hello," Tootie said. This was just the way she dreamed it would be. She felt so brave and confident. "Can we please talk with Mara?"

"Or Leon," Joey added bravely. Tootie noticed that he tried his best to stand very tall.

Tootie smiled and continued, "Our pastor visited here this afternoon and he said that you have some medicine for my brother. He's really sick."

The Gypsies looked at each other and shook their heads, frowning. They didn't seem to understand a word that was being said. Finally one woman, who wore dangling sequin earrings and was wrapped around several times with a purple fringed shawl, swung her head toward one of the caravans. Then she pointed with her multiringed finger at the caravan and again nodded her head.

Tootie smiled, said "Thank you," and then walked over to the caravan and knocked boldly on the front door.

Joey stood a step behind.

Immediately the door opened and they both stared directly up into the face of the big man with the black bushy eyebrows and mustache who had hollered, "A feast! A feast!" over the poor porcupine.

"Oh," Tootie moaned under her breath and swayed slightly.

Joey caught her.

"Come." The large man greeted them and stood aside for them to enter. His enormous belly almost blocked the entrance. Then he began speaking in another language to the two women sitting at a table in the caravan—the same two women who had sat next to the bonfire and watched the Christmas tree being decorated.

Mara and Leon were nowhere in sight.

Tootie and Joey stepped cautiously around the man and were shocked by the bright colors, beauty, and pleasant odors which filled the room. The inside of the caravan was even prettier than the outside. Everything was tidy and in its place. The floor was covered with thick red carpet, and two iron beds with checkered bedspreads stood on either side of a large wooden wardrobe. Pictures of Bible characters and family pictures hung together on the walls, most of them in silver or tin frames. The winter sun, shining through the white lace curtains and reflecting off the red carpet, gave everything a rosy appearance. It was as if they had stepped into another world.

The old wrinkled woman held a long clay pipe between her lips and the scent of oak leaves filled the room with each puff of smoke. She barely looked up at the newcomers. She was sitting at a heavy wooden table next to the woman with the bulging bosom who was pouring tea into fine china cups. The younger woman held out a cup to Tootie and then offered one to Joey. She nodded for them to drink.

Tootie's hand quivered and the china cup shook precariously on its saucer.

"Don't drink," Joey whispered. "It might be p-poison."

Just then the burly man took his cup. Then to her and Joey's utter surprise he stuck his tongue straight out and curled it until it looked like a funnel. Tipping his cup, he poured the entire contents down the funneled tongue into his mouth. In one giant gulp, the cup was drained.

Tootie stared at the man and then at Joey. She felt a giggle starting to rise when she saw Joey's horrified expression. Quickly she stuck her tongue out and tried to funnel it. Tipping her cup, she attempted to pour the lukewarm tea through the funnel just as the man had done. She missed her mouth and spilled the tea down the front of her coat.

The Gypsy man threw his head back and laughed uproariously, and so did the two women. He then slapped Joey on the back and said, "Drink," motioning for Joey to try and down the tea in the same manner.

Joey nervously put the cup to his lips and took a quick sip.

The Gypsy man laughed again. His mustache twitched as he repeated the word, "*Gadje, Gadje, Gadje,*" and kept pointing at them.

Tootie didn't know what a "Gadje" was, but she guessed it meant people like her and Joey—people who were not Gypsies. She could tell that he thought they were very strange indeed.

Then Tootie put her cup on the table and began to explain. "We have come for some medicine for my brother, Buddy. He's got a bad cold and our pastor told us you have medicine that will help him get better."

The Gypsy man went to the door and yelled something which Tootie could not understand. Within seconds Mara and Leon came into the caravan. Mara was even more beautiful than Tootie remembered. Her copper-colored skin looked flawless and she smiled, showing straight white teeth.

Her twin brother, Leon, stood by her side. His black hair was greased and combed neatly. His upper lip looked fuzzy with dozens of short black hairs. Tootie thought he looked surprisingly grown-up and she knew that someday he would have a fine mustache.

Finally Mara spoke. "This . . . Leon, you saw before."

Tootie and Joey nodded toward Leon. Tootie wanted to thank him for finding Buddy, but she felt nervous and tongue-tied.

Then Mara motioned proudly toward the big man, "This . . . Father. He head of *kumpama.*"

Tootie remembered that Pastor Myers had said that "kumpama" meant clan or group, and she knew that this big man was the one in charge of the Gypsies.

Then Mara indicated the buxom woman and said, "Mother." She came and stood next to the woman and put her dainty hand on her mother's shoulder. Leaning over, she kissed her mother's cheek and then the cheek of the old woman.

"This . . . Grandmother," Mara said reverently.

The old woman leaned forward and brushed her pale, thin lips tenderly against Mara's hair.

Tootie nodded in wonder to each one. They were so different from anything she had ever imagined. She felt almost overwhelmed in their presence. "Medicine?" Tootie whispered, and she felt ashamed of herself when her voice came out in a high nervous squeak.

Mara smiled and picked up a fancy covered jar. "This fat from hedgehog. You call porcupine. Rub on chest." And Mara moved her hand round and round in circles over her chest to demonstrate what she meant.

Tootie and Joey stared at each other. Finally Joey mouthed, "P-porcupine fat?"

Tootie felt blood rush to her face.

Then the Gypsy man handed Joey a sealed bottle filled to the top with green liquid. "Tea," he announced and pointed to their cups. Tootie realized it was some of the same tea they had been drinking. He funneled his tongue and pretended to pour the contents from the jar into his mouth.

Joey looked at Tootie and said sheepishly, "I th-think they are saying that Buddy should d-drink this."

Tootie almost felt like laughing. Joey looked so miserable.

The Gypsy man started talking rapidly in his own language to the two women and then he addressed Mara and Leon.

Leon spoke for the first time, "Father say we go with you. Help. We friends."

Tears stung Tootie's eyes. They really are friends. And they want to help. She knew people would stare, maybe even glare at them, when they walked down

Washington Street together. But she didn't care. *If these nice Gypsies want to help Buddy Boy, I'm not about to stop them.*

"Come," Tootie said. "We'd better hurry."

Joey didn't say a word. He just followed Tootie, Mara, and Leon away from the rosy glow of the caravan and out toward Washington Street.

Tootie, Joey and their new Gypsy friends reached the bakery without any trouble. No one had even looked their way. Washington Street was filled with people hurrying, a policeman with his whistle directing traffic, horns blaring, and trolley buses taking passengers home after a busy day.

Just when the four were about to ascend the outside steps leading up to the McCarthys' apartment, the bell on the bakery door jingled. Tootie held her breath and glanced over to the door of the Specialty Pie Bakery just a few feet away. To her horror Miss Penick and Mr. Harris started backing out. Totally preoccupied in their conversation with Tootie's father, they hadn't yet noticed Tootie or her friends. Tootie motioned frantically to Joey, Mara, and Leon to keep quiet and crouch down so they wouldn't be seen.

"It's going to be simply marvelous, Mr. McCarthy!" Miss Penick was saying.

"Yes, I'm sure the Christmas play will go well again this year," Donald commented. He was standing inside the bakery and hadn't seen Tootie or the others either. Then he said something which made Tootie feel like her heart had dropped down into her toes. "And I must admit, it has been a shock to hear such flowery praise about Tootie's angel costume."

Miss Penick responded in her loud, singsong voice, "As I said, Mr. McCarthy, we were all most surprised when your daughter described her outfit in such great detail this afternoon. It sounds simply divine. We are so anxious to see it, but I guess we'll have to wait until tomorrow!"

"Yes, yes, tomorrow!" Donald said, still bewildered over his daughter's lie. Tootie hadn't even mentioned that she was the head angel, much less that she needed a costume. Then Father continued, "And you say that my daughter even told you she planned to wear diamonds in her hair?"

"She certainly did," Mr. Harris interrupted with a wide grin. "It would be grand if all parents took this kind of interest in our school play. You are to be commended, Mr. McCarthy."

Tootie felt absolutely dreadful. How could this be happening? How could one lie be getting her into so much trouble? She looked at Joey's worried expression and then at her new friends, Mara and Leon. It was obvious they didn't know why they were trying to be quiet and hide on the stairway, but they nodded reassuringly at Tootie.

Tootie heard her father clear his throat and say solemnly, "Let me take this opportunity to thank you,

Mr. Harris, for the large order of tarts you've just placed. My wife and I will have them ready by Friday evening for Superintendent Henry's reception."

Tootie was desperate to escape. She definitely didn't want to face Father after he'd caught her lying about her angel costume, and she certainly didn't want any of them to see the Gypsies, Mara and Leon. "Hurry!" she whispered to her friends and motioned for them to tiptoe up the stairs.

Joey began leading the way. They had gone only a few steps when Mr. Harris glanced over his shoulder and saw them, "Confound it!" he shouted. "What do we have sneaking around here?"

The four young people stared down at the shocked expression of Principal Harris and the blanched face of Miss Penick.

Father looked around the bakery door and quickly took in the scene. "Gypsies, that's what we have. Our daughter and her friend, Joey Staddler, have brought Gypsies home for dinner. Now isn't that the Christian thing to do!"

Pure pride flooded Tootie's soul. Father always seemed to know what to say. And even if he were upset with her for lying about the angel costume or for bringing Gypsies home, he'd never let outsiders know.

"Introduce your friends, Tootie," Father said, and his whole face lit up with sudden mischief. He was beginning to enjoy the unexpected encounter because it was obvious Miss Penick and Mr. Harris were absolutely appalled by the Gypsies' presence. Miss Penick kept inhaling great gulps of air, and it sounded as if she were gagging on something extremely distasteful.

Tootie said nervously, "Mara and Leon, this is my father."

Mara bowed her head respectfully, while Leon stepped down off the stairs and shook hands.

"Welcome," Donald McCarthy said with exaggerated emphasis.

Tootie thought the silver buttons on Leon's jacket and his small silver earring were a thousand times more noticeable than ever before. They caught the reflection from inside the bakery and literally sparkled with dancing light.

Tootie nervously coughed and then said, "Mara and Leon, this is our school principal and my teacher, Miss Penick."

Leon stretched out his hand toward Mr. Harris, whose eyebrows shot up so high they were lost somewhere under his hat. He refused to shake Leon's hand and wouldn't even look at Mara.

Instead, he and Miss Penick turned on their heels and stormed away. Tootie thought she heard the principal mumbling something about both the Irish and the Gypsies needing to be run out of town. But she couldn't hear him clearly because of Miss Penick's ridiculous sounding gasps.

Tootie sputtered, "They make me so mad! Why do they have to be so rude?" She thought she saw raw anger flash momentarily across Father's Irish eyes.

"No matter," Mara said softly and tried her best to smile. "People always rude to Gypsies."

"But th-that's not right," Joey interrupted, forgetting his own previous rudeness. "H-how can you stand it?"

With a shake of his head, Leon said, "Fear of Gypsy magic dies hard."

"Oh, no!" Tootie interrupted, suddenly remembering Buddy. "We've got to get this medicine to my brother," and she held up the jar, filled with porcupine fat.

"And this," Joey added, and lifted the sealed jar of green tea. He stuck his tongue out funnel-fashion and pretended to pour the green liquid down his throat, making gasping, gulping noises just as Miss Penick had made.

Everyone laughed, even Father.

Then Donald looked at Tootie and said, "We'll talk about that mysterious angel costume later. But for now, you'd better go help your mother with Buddy."

He sounded stern, but Tootie knew he would not stay angry. He'd never lifted a hand to her in all her life. Her only fear was that she'd lose some of his respect because she had lied.

"Run along, Tootie," Father continued. "It's cold out here without my coat, and I have a few more things to do before I can close shop." And then he mumbled, "It's strange that Pearl hasn't come to help," as he closed the bakery door.

The following hour or two seemed to pass in a haze. Joey ran across the street to ask permission to stay at the McCarthy's. And to her total surprise, Mother was more accepting of the Gypsies than Tootie had ever dreamed possible. At first she was a little skeptical of the porcupine fat, but even that was eventually allowed. And she thanked them for their thoughtfulness in bringing the herb tea.

Buddy's fever was still high and he didn't wake up enough to recognize the Gypsies. He fought the spooning of the tea, but didn't mind his chest being rubbed with the animal fat. He kept saying over and over, "Toooootie . . . Toooootie."

In all the commotion, Tootie hadn't even missed Pearl.

Finally Mother commented, "Pearl's never been so late. It's almost six o'clock, and I'm getting worried."

Tootie stared at Joey and then back at Mother. "Pearl said she was going to stay after school. Maybe she's still there?"

"Gracious, lass, at this hour?"

"We'll go f-find her," Joey offered and swung into his coat.

Mara and Leon had been sitting on the edge of Buddy's bed. They jumped up and said in unison, "We help."

Eve wrung her hands, "I guess it would be all right. Go directly to the school and then come straight back. You understand? Stay in a group . . . all four of you."

"Come on," Tootie said as she grabbed for her coat and scarf. "Let's go find my sister."

As the young teenagers headed down Washington

Street looking everywhere for Pearl, Tootie found it easy to tell her new Gypsy friends about her sister. She told them all about how Pearl had taken up with the street preacher and her depression during the past days.

Mara and Leon were good listeners and before Tootie realized it she was confiding in them about the Christmas play and her need for an angel costume.

"That's right," Joey added, "and I have to c-come up with something that will lift Tootie high into the air. Our teacher wants it to look like Tootie is f-flying across the stage."

"We help," Leon said. "Gypsy good at lifting."

Before Tootie could say any more, they had reached the school. And for the moment, the only thing on Tootie's mind was finding her sister. "Pearl!" Tootie shouted over and over with all her might. "Pearl, where are you?"

The school was locked and dark. There were a few street lamps shining outside: one at the front entrance, one near the baseball field, and a third on the side of the building. Tootie, Joey, Mara, and Leon circled the school several times, but Pearl was nowhere in sight. And there was absolutely no way for them to get inside the building to take a closer look.

Suddenly Tootie had an idea and she motioned for everyone to be quiet. "I think I know where she is," Tootie whispered. "I don't know why I didn't think of it before. Remember, Joey, how Pearl always stands by that fence and stares at Banjo Ed while he does his construction work?"

Joey nodded.

"Well, I have this feeling that Pearl's over there," and Tootie pointed to the construction site on the other side of the fence.

"But it's d-dark over there," Joey complained. "How can we see anything? If we could only g-get into the school we could use my spotlights—the ones I brought for the play."

Tootie looked at the gas lamp on the tall pole at the side of the building. It was dirty and the light was dim. "What about that? Do you think we could wipe it off so it shines brighter? Then maybe we could see over there?" Tootie pointed to the construction site.

"Gypsy can," Mara said and motioned to her brother. Before another word could be said, Leon shinnied up the pole.

Tootie took off her red scarf, rubbed it in the snow to make it damp, and threw it up at him. After several tries, Leon caught the scarf. He made swift movements across the hot glass of the lamp, causing it to sizzle.

Everyone stared over toward the construction area. The scene which greeted them made Tootie's knees go weak. "Pearl!" she screamed. "What's happened to Pearl?"

Pearl lay sprawled, face down in the slushy snow. She was lying beside a pile of logs near a small construction shed. Some logs had rolled off the stack and were scattered around Pearl's body, with two large ones lying crisscross over her back.

Tootie ran toward the fence which separated the construction site from the school. The lock on the gate was hanging loose. She and Joey pushed open the heavy gate and kept running. Mara and Leon were close behind.

Tootie fell to her knees and quickly brushed aside Pearl's black hair, crying, "Pearl! Pearl!"

Pearl's face looked deathly white, but she opened her eyes. "I knew you would come," Pearl whispered and then shivered violently.

"Hurry," Tootie screamed. "Get these off her!"

With Joey and Leon's help, Tootie quickly removed the logs, while Mara took off her heavy shawl and covered Pearl.

"Pearl," Tootie said again and got down in the snow, close to her sister. "Can you move?"

Pearl whispered, "I think so," and she wiggled her toes and lifted her head. "Oh, Tootie, I'm so cold!"

Tootie took off her coat and put it on top of Mara's thick purple shawl.

"We've got to g-get her home," Joey said, "Why don't we roll her onto one of the s-shortest and f-flattest logs we can find. We'll use it like a stretcher to carry her home."

"You don't need to do that," Pearl countered, weakly.

"Shush," Tootie soothed. She tried her best to sound calm, but her heart was racing.

"I . . . I was climbing up there," Pearl tried to explain as she pointed to the pile of logs. "Everything kept sliding down on me."

"Hush now," Tootie demanded. "You can tell us all about it later." She couldn't imagine why in the world Pearl was trying to climb up a pile of logs.

"I prayed you'd come," Pearl said simply and closed her eyes.

Tootie, Joey, Mara, and Leon worked together and carefully moved Pearl onto a log about the same length as Pearl. Tootie reached for her scarf, which was stuffed into the pocket of Leon's baggy pants, and hurriedly threaded it under the log. Then she pulled the ends of the scarf together to tie them into a knot over Pearl's tummy. "This is going to keep you from running away from us," Tootie said, trying her best to sound lighthearted.

Pearl whispered, "No more running away . . . I promise."

Tootie wasn't sure if she heard her sister correctly. "You're going to be all right, Pearl. I just know it!" she whispered back.

Pearl opened her eyes again and for the first time in weeks there was a calm, almost peaceful expression on her face. She smiled up at Tootie and Joey and then into the wide, black eyes of Mara and Leon. She didn't even look surprised that they were helping her. Then she closed her eyelids and visibly relaxed as if she were resting in the care of ministering angels.

It was dark as the four carried Pearl home. The log was heavy and they had to stop several times. It seemed strange, almost unreal, to be walking silently down Washington Street holding the makeshift stretcher, listening to Pearl's deep breathing. Most of her shivers were gone and it looked as though she had fallen asleep.

Father and Mother had been waiting by the front door. When Eve saw the small procession coming toward the bakery, she cried, "My baby! What's happened to my baby?" She and Father came running down the stairs.

Pearl woke. "Oh, Mama . . . Daddy!"

"Hush, lass," Father said. "Just rest."

Tootie quickly told her parents where they had found Pearl and that they didn't think she had any broken bones. Father untied the scarf and very tenderly picked Pearl up in his arms. He carried her up the steps and into the bedroom. He gently laid her in bed, as the others gathered around.

"Oh," Pearl sighed as she settled into the saggy mattress, "this feels so good." She stretched full-length.

Tootie leaned over and hugged her sister.

"Maybe you shouldn't move so much, Pearl," Mother said anxiously. "We're going to send for a doctor and have you examined."

Pearl sneezed. "I'll be all right, Mama. Honest. I'm just cold."

"We're taking no chances," Father reassured. "You may only feel tired and cold tonight, but believe me, tomorrow you'll be mighty stiff and sore."

Pearl looked up at her parents. "I couldn't budge because of those logs, and I thought I was going to freeze to death. I was so scared!"

"Anybody would be s-scared," Joey said.

"Of course they would," Tootie added and piled more blankets on top of her sister.

Pearl sneezed several more times. "But I prayed," Pearl added. "And in my heart I just knew someone would come to save me."

"You brave," Leon said.

"You brave like Gypsy," Mara added.

"Which reminds me," Mother interrupted, "where is that herbal tea?"

"Here," Joey said as he reached for the bottle of green tea and handed it to Mr. and Mrs. McCarthy, who were sitting on the edge of the bed next to Pearl.

While Mother helped Pearl drink, Father said, "Let me ask you, lass. What were you doing out there? What in blazes were you thinking of when you went into that construction area?"

Pearl answered honestly, "Banjo Ed." Then she took another sip of tea.

"That old boyfriend of yours?" Mother asked, stunned. "I thought we'd heard the last of him. Now why in the world—"

"Let the lass explain," Father broke in, and got up and walked over to lean against the door.

Everyone waited.

After a moment Pearl began her story about how lonely and hurt she'd been after her breakup with Banjo Ed. She went on to explain that he was now working at the construction site and she had decided to go over after school and talk with him.

"He laughed at me," Pearl said quietly and her face turned even more pale. "Then he—he took out some money and teased me. He told all the rest of the workmen that I wanted to get my teeth fixed and that I needed money for a dentist." She lowered her head and said the rest barely above a whisper. "He threw the coins into the pile of wood and told me to fetch them."

Tootie could hear her father shuffle his feet, but she didn't dare look up because she was trying to deal with her own anger over Banjo Ed. *How dare he treat my sister like that!*

Pearl continued, "I hid in the shed until all the men were gone, and then I tried to find the money. I guess that's when it happened."

"So that's why you were climbing up there!" Tootie

interrupted. "That man makes me sick! Oh, Pearl, why do you put up with him?"

"No more!" Pearl said, and she looked like she meant it. "I never want to see him again. *Ever!* Lying there under the logs with my face in the snow I had time to think. I've been such a fool! I don't understand why I ever liked him."

"I could never understand that either," Father said as he shuffled his feet again.

"Donald!" Eve admonished.

"Well, it's the truth. And I'm glad Pearl's finally come to her senses. I'm just sorry she had to go through so much to discover it."

"That's enough talk," Mother said. "I want all of you to leave the room so I can rub some porcupine fat on Pearl's chest."

"Porcupine fat!" Pearl squealed.

"Yes, porcupine fat," Mother said with a smile. "We've learned some new home remedies from our Gypsy friends."

Mara, who had been standing quietly by the dresser next to her twin brother, stepped forward. "It works," she said proudly and pointed at Buddy who was waking up.

"Gyps . . . Gyps!" Buddy said and clapped his chubby hands.

Everyone laughed. The tension of the last few hours had passed.

Tootie rushed over to her brother's bed. "Oh, Buddy Boy, you're better!"

"And Pearl will soon be better too," Father said with a mischievous look. "If you'd all leave the room so my wife can administer that porcupine fat."

"Oh, Daddy, don't let her," Pearl said, and pulled the covers over her head.

Everyone laughed again.

The four young people quickly left the room. Mara and Leon had to get back to their Gypsy camp, but as they stood by the doorway in the McCarthy apartment, Leon hesitated. "Gypsy treated same way," Leon said.

Tootie knew what he meant. It was obvious that Joey also understood.

Mara said, "Gypsy can't go to school. Chase away!"

"What can we do?" Tootie asked. She looked at her new Gypsy friends and then at Joey. "We've got to do something! They should be able to go to school if they want to."

Joey hesitated and then he said, "We're in enough t-trouble. Remember?"

Immediately Tootie remembered the Christmas play and her awful lie.

"Gypsies . . . much white curtain." Mara stretched her arms out wide to show they had lots and lots of the lacy white curtain material.

"You would give me some of your beautiful white lace for my angel costume?" Tootie asked. She knew it would make a heavenly costume. Her heart began to race.

Mara nodded her head and smiled. Her straight white teeth gleamed bright in her beautiful golden-colored face. "Gypsies love jewels." She touched her many strands of beads. "We find necklace—put here," and she pretended to string diamonds in Tootie's curly hair.

"Oh," Tootie mouthed. She felt all choked up.

Then Leon added, "Horse harness. Lift angel." He flung his arms high into the air. "Fly!" and he moved his arms back and forth over his head.

Tootie and Joey looked at each other.

"It just m-might work," Joey said excitedly.

"Do you really think so?" Tootie asked.

They both remembered the horse harnesses and bells which they had seen the first time they discovered the Gypsy camp.

"Your legs fit through the harness," Leon explained. "You sit. Put long straps on harness and . . . and . . ."

"And attach those leather straps to the big curtain rod high up at the b-back of the stage," Joey added. "You know—there are some up there for b-backdrops."

Tootie nodded.

"We could fix something up so it w-works like a pulley," Joey went on. "It'll work, Tootie. You're going to f-fly!"

"Fly!" Leon added confidently and again swung his arms back and forth.

Tootie could almost see it. She was flying through the air, high above the stage, in a beautiful white lace dress with sparkles in her hair and bells ringing. It was even better than she ever imagined.

Later that night, as Tootie lay in bed next to Pearl,

she thought back over the events of the past weeks and an immense feeling of thankfulness flooded over her. God had been at work all along, even if she hadn't recognized it. God was there when Pearl needed him even when she was pinned down in the snow. He had used her and Joey and the Gypsies to find Pearl.

And God had helped Buddy. He may have used herbal tea and porcupine fat, but God was there.

And now God had even made a way for her to have an angel costume.

"You really do care, don't you," Tootie whispered into her pillow. "Oh, Father in heaven, I'm so sorry I lied! I wish I had trusted you." A tear escaped and soaked into her pillowcase.

Just then an idea popped into her mind—a fantastic idea! Mr. Harris would be shocked and Miss Penick just might faint—not to mention Superintendent Henry and a multitude of parents. But for some reason, she knew this surprising idea had come from God.

By the next morning, Pearl had indeed come down with a bad cold and was stiff and sore as Father had predicted. The doctor came and pronounced she had no broken bones. But what pleased the McCarthy family even more was that Pearl's depression was finally gone. Except for her terrible bruises and the worst cold she'd ever had, Pearl was back to her old self.

But now Pearl and Buddy both needed tending, so Tootie stayed home the rest of the week to help. Mother had to work in the bakery and assist with the large order of tarts for Superintendent Henry's reception. All of this added to Miss Penick's frustration. She wanted her head angel to attend play practices.

Each day Mara and Leon came to the apartment to visit. They brought more herbal tea, porcupine fat, and even a swatch of the beautiful lace material from the Gypsy camp. Mara's mother and grandmother insisted on sewing the angel dress. They also sent a message that they were sewing long strips of material to wind around and cover the leather straps of the harness so that Tootie would appear as if she were truly flying.

Leon had loaned the harness to Joey, who promptly took it to school to the delight of Miss Penick. She, of course, did not know it was a harness from one of the Gypsy horses.

Over and over again Joey tried to reassure Miss Penick that all would go well in spite of Tootie's absence from rehearsals. He brought a piece of the material from her angel dress to prove the existence of the costume, and he also promised he would coach Tootie on her lines.

Every afternoon Joey came over and joined Tootie, Mara, and Leon. Tootie recited her script from Luke, chapter two: "Fear not; for, behold, I bring you good tidings of great joy, which shall be to all people." Tootie went on with the entire salutation, finishing with the words: "Ye shall find the babe wrapped in swaddling clothes, lying in a manger."

But every chance Tootie had to be alone, she worked on the plan God had given her the night they found Pearl. She hadn't told anyone about this fantastic idea because she wanted to have everything ready and make it a total surprise.

Finally Friday afternoon arrived. Joey was already at Tootie's when Mara and Leon hurried up the apartment steps. When Tootie opened the door to let them in, the Gypsy twins greeted her with the most beautiful white dress she had ever seen in all her life. The Gypsies had designed an angel costume which almost took her breath away. The scalloped neckline was threaded with layer after layer of pearl-colored sequins. The sleeves were big and puffy at the shoulders and narrowed at the wrists. Below a fitted waistline, the skirt flowed out with yards of soft white lace. The floor-length hem was scalloped to match the neckline, and Mara's mother had meticulously sewn rows of more pearl-colored sequins along its edge.

"Oh! It's beautiful!" Tootie exclaimed. "I never imagined it would look this pretty!"

Joey, who never paid much attention to dresses, also thought it was beautiful. "Those sh-shiny things will really show up when I put the s-spotlight on you."

"This shine too," Leon said and brought out from behind his back a circle of diamonds strung on a wire frame.

"Oh!" Tootie gasped. "I can't believe it!"

"Diamonds not real," Leon said. "They fake."

"They're beautiful!"

Leon pointed to the frame. "Father made."

Tootie couldn't imagine the big Gypsy man with the bushy eyebrows and mustache making such a delicate thing.

"Mother's necklace," Mara said and pointed to the string of diamonds.

Tootie was totally overcome with emotion. She closed her eyes, hugging the angel dress to her heart. Her dream had come true; her prayers were answered. *Oh God,* she prayed silently, *thank you!*

Then she opened her eyes and with tears clouding her vision looked at Mara and Leon. "Thank you. And please thank your parents for me," she said. "You are all such special friends."

Mara smiled. "Here," and took the halo, placing it on Tootie's head. The wire frame settled down into Tootie's soft brown curls and disappeared from sight. The circle of diamonds stuck up above her head like a real halo.

"Look in a mirror!" Joey said. "You w-won't believe it! It actually l-looks like a real halo!"

The four teenagers hurried into the bedroom to show Pearl and Buddy, but they were nowhere in sight. The beds were strewn with old robes and strips of material that had been sewn together into long multicolored sashes.

"What's all this?" Joey asked.

Tootie halted on her way to the mirror. This wasn't the way she had planned it. "These are shepherd costumes for tonight," she admitted reluctantly. And then she carefully laid her angel dress down on the bed next to them.

"You made?" Mara asked, picking up one of the costumes.

Suddenly Tootie felt embarrassed. "Yes," she admitted. "I'm not very good at sewing. Anyway, I got every scrap of material I could find in the house, and then I sewed them all together. This is a sash," and she pointed to the one Mara was holding. "It can be worn around the waist or draped over the shoulder like this." Tootie flung the sash over Mara's slender shoulder. "Or it could be wrapped around the head like a turban. I think the sashes sort of spruce up these old bathrobes."

"I like!" Leon said and dramatically swung one

around his neck, looping the end over his head and down to his shoulder.

Mara held another up to her face so that only her black, mysterious-looking eyes peered over the top.

Tootie and Joey laughed. Finally Joey said, "I didn't know Miss Penick asked you to make costumes for the sh-shepherds. She hasn't mentioned a word about it. Wh-who are they for?"

Tootie took a deep breath. "They're for Mara and Leon."

After a startled silence, Joey asked "*Who?*"

"You heard me," Tootie laughed. "The costumes are for Mara and Leon. I think they should dress up like shepherds and be the ones to hang onto the leather straps of the harness. You told me, Joey, that you've fixed it all up like a pulley. Someone's got to hold the leather straps. And that's going to be Mara and Leon. They're going to be the ones to work the pulley and help me fly across the stage.

"Oh, Tootie," Joey said, "that's p-perfect!"

"We cannot," Mara said sadly and dropped the crudely made sash onto the bed. "We Gypsies."

"We cannot go to school," Leon added. "People hate Gypsies."

"They're right," Joey admitted. "Miss Penick would have a f-fit and so would Mr. Harris. They'd never let G-Gypsies be in the school play."

"Just listen," Tootie interrupted. "Mara and Leon can dress up in these robes and wrap the sashes around their head with only their eyes showing. No one will notice them because everyone will be so busy, and most of us will already be in costumes."

She paused and looked at Mara's and Leon's hopeful expressions. "After the play begins, when it's my turn to come on stage, you two just rearrange your sashes and smile real big. You'll make perfect shepherds! And by that time it'll be too late for anyone to do anything about it."

Soon Tootie and Joey were helping Mara and Leon into their shepherd costumes. When they wrapped the sashes around their waists, shoulders, and heads, Joey said, "You know, this just m-might work! You look great!"

Tootie thought they looked like real shepherds from centuries ago; their golden skin adding to the illusion. She could almost hear the sheep and see the lush green hills around Bethlehem.

"I scared!" Mara admitted.

"Me, too," Leon said. "But I want to be in play."

Mara turned and looked directly at Tootie. "I too want to be in play about baby Jesus. We like baby Jesus story."

"Well," Tootie said, "I think it's high time you were included in the Christmas play at Logan School. Don't you, Joey?"

"I sure do," Joey said with confidence.

Tootie smiled at him and then at her Gypsy friends. "Come on. We've got to hurry. I want to put on my angel dress and then we have to get to school before anyone else arrives."

"That's right," Joey added. "And I want to p-practice shining my spotlight on all three of you—so hurry up and g-get dressed, Tootie."

"How can I with you two standing there!" Tootie quickly shooed Joey and Leon out of the bedroom. With Mara's help, she slipped into the angel dress. Then she stood in front of the mirror. "Is that me?" she asked in surprise. "Is that really me?"

Mara giggled. "Tootie pretty."

She had never felt pretty before. In fact, she had always thought of herself as a short, flat, very plain girl. But the girl staring back at her was anything but plain.

With nimble fingers, Mara skillfully combed Tootie's hair and replaced the halo. Then she applied a small amount of Pearl's pink lipstick to Tootie's trembling lips.

Tootie turned to take one last long look in the mirror, and then she and Mara hurried out of the bedroom.

"Wow!" Joey said, the moment he saw Tootie.

"Pretty!" Leon announced. "Pretty as a Gypsy girl!"

Tootie wasn't used to compliments. At first she felt self-conscious but then she raised her arms and gracefully danced around the room, pretending to be an angel bestowing blessings with a touch of her finger on the top of each head.

Everyone was laughing when Tootie's parents came into the apartment. Pearl and Buddy were with them. Donald, Eve, and Pearl each carried a large box of tarts ready for the reception.

"Oh, gracious me!" Tootie's mother exclaimed. "You look beautiful!"

"My little lass!" Donald said, and then he smiled at Tootie, obviously taking great delight in the transformation of his youngest daughter.

Pearl was completely awed by the dress, and Buddy kept touching the shiny sequins and saying, "Ooooo! Ooooo!"

In the midst of all the excitement, Tootie tried her best to explain why Mara and Leon were dressed in shepherd costumes. "I just know this idea of including them in the Christmas play came from God. I honestly think God's the one who popped it into my brain."

"In that case, Tootie," Mother admitted, "it's got to work!"

Donald looked thoughtful. "Why don't you two invite your parents and the rest of the caravan to come?" he suggested. "I'm sure they'll all want to see you in your first school play."

"That's right," Eve added. "And they will also want to see this pretty angel dress on Tootie. After all their hard work, it would be a shame if they didn't come."

About an hour later all was ready. Mara and Leon had practiced moving Tootie up and down and across the school stage in the harness which was attached to the pulley high above. And Joey had learned just where to shine the spotlights. It was time to hide Mara and Leon before the others started arriving.

Tootie found a place for them in the folds of the heavy stage curtain, over in a corner. They were to come out only after the lights were low and the play had begun.

The very second that Mara and Leon were tucked

out of sight, students began to arrive. Everyone was in costume, but Tootie became the center of attention. Even Irene, the girl in her beautiful Mary costume, was obviously shocked at Tootie's appearance.

Finally Miss Penick rushed in. "You did come after all!" she said. Her long nose was red and she kept shaking her head as she talked. "But I must say, this gorgeous dress and that magnificent halo of yours has redeemed you. This is certainly better than any costume we've ever had in our Christmas play!"

Principal Harris came up to join Miss Penick behind the stage to see if all was going well. He too complimented Tootie's dress and went on to inspect the lace-covered harness. "Most ingenious! This will certainly enhance the show. Who's going to pull these?" he asked and lifted up the leather straps which Mara and Leon would use.

Tootie didn't know how to answer. Lies had certainly gotten her into enough trouble already, and she wasn't about to repeat the same mistake.

Just then there was a loud commotion from the auditorium. Mr. Harris and Miss Penick poked their heads around the drawn curtain to see what was the matter.

"Gypsies!" they both gasped, and Tootie thought she saw both of their bodies go limp.

At that very moment, Superintendent Henry arrived backstage. He was tall and looked very distinguished in his dark suit and neatly trimmed black mustache. Mr. Harris and Miss Penick began to stutter and stammer, obviously trying to stall so that Superintendent

Henry wouldn't peer through the curtains and spot the crowd of Gypsies.

"Let's go sit down in the front," Mr. Harris said, obviously in great distress. His eyebrows shot up higher than ever before and kept quivering in place. He grasped a firm hold of Superintendent Henry's arm and led him away.

"Your attendance is an honor," Miss Penick said as she fluttered after them.

As soon as they left, Tootie peeked out. Indeed, the Gypsies had arrived. All of them!

Everyone else in the auditorium seemed shocked, all except the McCarthys and Pastor Myers. Tootie noticed that Pearl and Buddy were talking to the old Gypsy grandmother who held her unlit pipe between her lips. The confusion that the Gypsies created among the rest of the parents, teachers, and students was close to pandemonium.

Suddenly the lights lowered and everyone began scrambling to their seats.

Tootie ran over to the corner and motioned for Mara and Leon to come out and take their places. They firmly held the leather straps and Tootie climbed into the harness. The other actors and actresses rushed to their places on stage without noticing the two strangers in their midst.

The curtain opened and the play began.

One scene followed another. All the ninth grade students were doing great except Irene, who kept forgetting her lines.

The choir sang beautifully, and before Tootie realized it they were singing the carol, "While Shepherds Watched Their Flocks." She knew this was her cue. The moment they finished the last word to the carol, she was to be lifted high in her harness and Joey would shine the stoplight directly on her, Mara, and Leon.

Suddenly doubts flooded over Tootie. *Have I made a mistake? Is this really what God had in mind? What's the crowd going to do when the spotlight encircles me and the Gypsies?*

Finally the last note died away, and Mara and Leon started pulling on the leather straps. Tootie went higher and higher. Panic began strangling her. And then to her horror, she realized she could not remember one word she was supposed to say. Her mind went totally blank.

At that very moment the spotlight engulfed her. The audience literally gasped at the brilliance and beauty of the sparkling light as it reflected off the sequins and halo.

Then Mara and Leon started to pull Tootie across the stage to make it appear as if she were flying. At that point Joey doubled the lights so that they encircled not only Tootie, but also Mara and Leon.

"Gypsies!" someone yelled. "Gypsies are on stage!"

It looked as if the whole audience began to move. Some stretched to get a closer look; others rose to their feet; a few stormed out.

All too soon the last chord of the music died down and the tense audience waited. Tootie's heart pounded. All she wanted to do was jump down out of the harness and run away. Then she heard Leon whisper, "Fear not . . . fear not."

"Fear not!" Tootie repeated. In her nervousness she shouted so loudly that her words vibrated round and round the auditorium. "Fear not," she repeated again. "For, behold, I bring you good tidings of great joy, which shall be to all people. . . ."

While Tootie said her lines, Mara and Leon moved back and forth across the stage with Tootie flying far above them. The audience seemed spellbound.

Then the spotlight moved away from Tootie and the Gypsies and focused on the manger scene.

As the drama came to a close and the choir finished their final song, the crowd rose to their feet clapping and cheering. Tootie had never heard anything like it. She looked down at Leon and Mara. They looked up and smiled. Leon's earring picked up the light and sparkled boldly for all to see. Tootie had never felt so happy.

To everyone's surprise, Superintendent Henry left his place and hurried up to the stage. The parents quieted down immediately to hear what he had to say.

"Let me take this opportunity to commend Mr. Harris, your fine principal, and your excellent teacher, Miss Penick, for this grand performance."

Everyone clapped again.

Superintendent Henry waved his hands. "But beyond this, let me commend them for including the young people from the Gypsy band as shepherds."

The crowd became restless. In the front row Mr. Harris and Miss Penick appeared completely dumbfounded.

"What fine examples you've been," the superintendent continued. "You have shown everyone the true meaning of Christmas. You have not only invited the Gypsies to attend, but you have included two of them in your school performance."

Miss Penick looked as if she had shrunk three inches.

Then Superintendent Henry said something even more shocking, "*I* am a Gypsy. But because of prejudice, I have kept this fact a secret for many years. You wonderful people have given me renewed courage."

Tootie tried her best to stifle her giggles when she saw the horrified expressions of the principal and Miss Penick. "Now without further ado," Superintendent Henry shouted with his hands high in the air, "Let's eat!"

Tootie thought he looked remarkably like Mara's and Leon's father as he stood by the bonfire announcing a feast over the poor porcupine.

Tootie remembered Pastor Myers' comment: "God works in mysterious ways." *He certainly does,* she thought.

"Come," Mara and Leon said excitedly as they lowered Tootie and began helping her climb out of the harness. "Let's go see Gypsy Henry!"

Tootie agreed. "But then let's find Joey and Buddy Boy. I'm dying to eat some of my parents' porcupine—I mean tarts!"

They all burst into laughter.